**People had been** 
**Devil's Elbow, Ke**▮▮▮▮▮**,** ▮▮▮ **over 60**
**years. On July 4ᵗʰ, 1971, they all came**
**walking out of the Ohio River.**

Sixteen-year-old Cadillac witnesses a Bible-camp bus
plunge off mountainous Devil's Elbow Road into the
Ohio River. The next day, July 4ᵗʰ, 1971, Cadillac
and other local residents witness the emergence of
The Dead from the river—not just the children
from the bus, one of whom is Cadillac's secret crush,
but dozens of people who have disappeared over the
past six decades. Devil's Elbow is a town with its
share of horrors, even without Dead people walking
out of the river, and residents are divided in how
they see The Dead. Some see gruesome walking
corpses. Others see normal, beautiful loved ones.
Conflicts build between those who accept The Dead
and those who want them gone. Soon The Dead
discover they cannot sleep and have no desire for
food—not until a terrifying hunger overcomes them.
Cadillac, looking back from fifty years later,
describes the horrific and redeeming events that
follow.

Spencer proves once again that he is a master story-
teller. *An Untimely Frost* will keep you up late, first
to finish it, then to think about it! It has all the
glorious gore of a true horror novel, but there is
much more that lies beneath. This book will leave
you asking yourself: What is real? What is merely
perceived reality? Does true love last forever? Don't
miss this one!—*Rhonda G. Williams, author of Girl
Brown*

i

An innovation for the fresh generation of readers looking for a new *Walking Dead*, but it is also so beautifully written that an old lady like me can dig it.—*Cherri Randall, author of One Vanilla Orchid*

If you think you know the Dead, think again. Mark Spencer weaves an artful tale of colorful, fresh, and horrific characters (think Faulkner, Serling, and King) in his coming-of-age book. An original and beautiful story of life, death and romance—in that order.—*R. L. Gemmill, author of Doomsday*

A spooky page-turner with more twists and turns than a mountain highway! — *Sylvia Ann McLain, author of Spinning Jenny*

Mark Spencer's breathtaking new novel, *An Untimely Frost,* is many things—a Southern horror story, a love story, a commentary on what divides us—but mostly it's the tangled adventure of sixteen-year-old Cadillac as he navigates through deaths and awakenings in his cloistered hometown, Devil's Elbow. Mark has masterfully combined colorful prose with a fast-paced plot to create a novel I simply couldn't put down. I read it in one sitting.—*Rich Marcello, author of The Beauty of the Fall*

Mark Spencer's novel *An Untimely Frost* surprises and delights. It's a horror story combined with romance, a coming-of-age story spiced with humor. At the same time, profound themes emerge: the nature of reality, the complexities of relationships, traditional vs. alternate views of life after death. An entertaining and thought-provoking read.—*Constance McKee, author of the Girl in the Mirror.*

*An Untimely Frost* is a gripping brew of horror and humor, love and hunger--with unexpected chilling twists and a creepy but oddly satisfying ending.— *Dawn Lajeunesse, author of In Her Mother's Shoes and Autumn Colors*

*An Untimely Frost* features vividly drawn characters in a deeply atmospheric setting. It really grabbed me. Vivid and chilling.—*Barbara Barnett, Bram Stoker Award Finalist, author of The Apothecary's Curse and The Alchemy of Glass.*

Mark Spencer's *An Untimely Frost* is a wickedly comic romp through the mythical community of Devil's Elbow on the Kentucky side of the Ohio River in the summer of 1971, when an itinerant preacher raises the dead from the river's depths. With Hitchcockian suspense and humor, Spencer navigates the reader through eternal questions of good and evil, spirit and flesh, and what we might actually do with our lives if gifted with immortality and a longing for love. Would we become gods or zombies? In 1971 only Jim Morrison could light the way.—*Steve Heller, author of The Automotive History of Lucky Kellerman, winner of the O. Henry Award and Friends of American Writers First Prize.*

*Praise for other fiction by Mark Spencer:*

"Grimly funny, to be sure, but funny, nevertheless."—*The Dallas Morning News*

iii

# An Untimely Frost

## Mark Spencer

Moonshine Cove Publishing, LLC
Abbeville, South Carolina U.S.A.
First Moonshine Cove edition October 2019

ISBN: 978-1-945181-702
Library of Congress PCN: 2019914723
Copyright© 2019 by Mark Spencer

Book cover design by Grady Earls; interior design by Moonshine Cove staff.

## About the Author

Mark Spencer is the author of *Ghost Walking,* four other novels, three collections of short stories, and a history book. He has won the Faulkner Society Faulkner Award for the Novel, the Omaha Prize for the Novel, the Bradshaw Book Award, and the Cairn Short Fiction Award. He and his family live in the famously haunted Allen House in Monticello, Arkansas.

"Death lies on her like an untimely frost."

*—Romeo and Juliet*

"I think science in our lifetime has a chance to conquer death. I think it's very possible."

*—Jim Morrison*

# AN UNTIMELY

# FROST

# BEFORE

*The Vanishings*

When I was a kid—a true child, not like now—I would sit on the veranda of my family's hill-perched, sagging mansion at night and watch the mist rise from the Ohio River. The mist was almost better than TV, the way it stretched and swirled into all kinds of entertaining shapes. Often it turned into long-fingered hands reaching up from a grave, then became the tentacles of a sci-fi-movie creature. The tentacles turned into dragons, the dragons into horses, the horses into cows. I would shout, "Mooooo!" into the darkness, and the sound carried across the valley and the river to the Ohio side.

A puff of breeze and the cows disintegrated, their fragments swirling, wafting, morphing into a dog upright on its hind legs and then into the Holy Ghost out for a stroll on the water.

A sudden and forlorn foghorn would blast and echo over the dark water. A speedboat's wasp-like motor whined in the distance. A paddle boat covered in colored lights sailed past like a mobile carnival. Tires and brakes screamed on nearby Devil's Elbow Road. An owl let out a hoot. A chunky toad splashed into the river. The tall grass and weeds on the steep hillside swayed with the slithering of raccoons and opossum and water moccasins.

A breeze might stir the mist into a griffin or a cyclops.

But it was just mist that arose from the water. All of those things I *thought* I saw, those illusions, were just mist.

Then came noon, July 4th, 1971, under the searing sun, when dead people walked out of that brown river.

*They* were real.

***

My father named me Cadillac. My sister, Peugeot, called herself Peggy because, as she said, "We ain't French," even though Mama thought "Peugeot" was a pretty name.

Our father wanted my middle name to be El Dorado, but Mama put her foot down and insisted on "Earl" after her father, the same as she insisted that Peugeot's middle name be Ethel after grandpa's sister.

Peggy might have eventually forgiven our father for naming her after a French car, but she never forgave him for vanishing. She was only three years older than I was, but she claimed to have a vivid recollection of the day he left us in August 1955.

The humidity lay like a hot towel over the world, she said. It was like most summer days when you lived on the river—suffocating. And of course our decrepit monstrosity of a house was full of flies. She said Bert—our father—kicked open the flimsy screen door and let it slap-bang at his back.

She told me the story so many times when we were kids that it eventually felt like my own memory.

He stooped at the rusty pump in the front yard, splashed water on his face, on his crew-cut, on the back of his red neck, and then wiped his hands on his baggy brown suit trousers. It was Sunday, and his church shoes were two-tone brown and white. A minute before, he and Mama had some spat in the kitchen.

She had said, "*Well?*"

And he said, "Jesus Christ!"

He noticed that rust had come off the pump handle onto his hand and he glared at his rust-bloody palm. Then he looked up and glared at his great-grandpa's slave-built mansion gone to rot, taking in the sagging porch roofs, the crumbling chimneys, the cockeyed weather vane on the south turret, the missing shingles, the cracked windows, the mold-blackened clapboards like bruises under the attic windows. The nineteenth-century tin roof tiles bled streaks of rust down the gray-weathered walls.

He spat, got in his car, and pulled the door closed hard. His car wasn't a Cadillac, not in the real world, but I always saw it as one in my made-up recollection. A chrome-smothered, two-tone red and white El Dorado.

Behind the big red-and-chrome steering wheel, he lit a cigarette with shaky hands. Then the car's engine exploded to life; the tires dug in; and a cloud of orange dust was left to settle as the sun set.

Peggy said I screamed like a stuck pig while Mama cradled me in her slim arms—I was only four months old—and muttered to me that Daddy would be back, as if I knew what was going on. Mama seemed unconcerned. She muttered, "I hope he remembers to get the Crisco."

Davis General Store opened up on Sundays against God's law, but plenty of church people bought from Mr. Davis anyway because people ate more on Sundays than they did other days—just like they drank more on Saturdays—and there was always a need for more flour or milk or sugar or Crisco oil.

After he didn't come back that night, Mama started sitting long hours on the sagging porch in a squeaky rocking chair, sitting up and peering at the sound of every car on our road. She spent the rest of the summer that way, tears glistening on her pale confused face. My sister said never to ask Mama about Bert unless I wanted to make Mama cry.

***

In the summer of 1971, as far as I could tell, Mama had long given up any hope that the mystery of my father's disappearance would be solved, much less any expectation that he would materialize at the front door, maybe in a new Sunday suit and freshly shaved, or that he would slip into the house in the middle of the night and ease into her bed to warm her backside.

People often disappeared from Devil's Elbow. His disappearance was just one in a series of vanishing acts among residents of our hamlet, the total population of which consisted of about three dozen families. Over the last sixty years or so, at least half of those families had had a member or two drop off the face of the earth.

There's no one there now, not a soul, as I tell this story nearly fifty years later. Devil's Elbow has been wiped out of existence, not even a dot on a map anymore.

In 1971, my sixteenth birthday fell on Easter, and Mama gave me ten dollars. I took the two five-dollar bills across the road to Miss Gertrude Trout. She was ninety-five years old and "a colored lady," as we said back then in that place. My great grandpa had owned her parents, but she never seemed to hold it against me.

She grew all kinds of herbs and spices and berries in her garden, and she spent a lot of time in the woods gathering things that grew wild. She made her living selling home remedies for anything that ailed a person, as well as potions for love, luck, and revenge. People said she was a witch, an agent of the Devil, but I noticed plenty of Baptists, Methodists, and "Frogs" pulling their cars up to her shack and coming away with small sacks or jars.

On my sixteenth birthday, I went to her clutching those five-dollar bills in my sweaty hand to buy a love potion to try on Kathy Mayhew, a girl at my high school. Miss Trout was very dark-skinned and shiny and had very pink gums and no teeth. Her toes were incredibly long, and her toenails were like yellowish talons. Her hair consisted of only a few steel-gray wires, and I could see most of her skull. From her porch rocker, she stared hard at my face for a long time while I fidgeted. She had only one good eye. The left one was all milky. The right one was green, which was another reason people said she was a witch— who ever heard of a colored person with a green eye?

The day I turned sixteen, that green eye skewered my soul.

Finally, she shook her head and smacked her gums. Then she reached into a pocket of her shift and pulled out a set of false teeth she had carved herself from teak wood and popped them in. "Boy, give me yo hand." I reached out my right hand. "Other one, boy." She peered at it, turned it, rubbed it, then dropped it like she'd discovered it to be of no more value than a dry dog turd. "Boy, you keeps that money. Now's not the time for you and that girl. The time'll come, but it ain't now."

I opened my mouth, but she stopped me like a traffic cop with her darkly lined pink palm. Her fingernails were long and yellow like her toenails and looked lethal.

"Don't be askin' me how I knows this."

So instead I asked, "How do love potions work?"

She cocked her head, and she sank that green eye of hers deep inside me. I could feel it poking around in my gut and then squeezing my heart and then measuring the size of my brain. "You really wanta know?"

"Yeah. I took chemistry last year. Is it something chemical?"

"Lordy, you's a scientist."

"I'm just wondering."

"I will tell yo, but don't go thinkin' you can make yo own. It won't work. The chem-o-stray of it is only a part."

And that was the beginning of her teaching me magic.

*** 

In the heat of the afternoons, Miss Trout would always rest on the wooden porch of her shack with a corncob pipe, and throughout that spring and into summer, she taught me about the magical and medicinal uses of tomato stems, apple cores, potato eyes, corn kernels, onion skins, various roots and herbs, black ants, red ants, fly wings, snake skins, frog tongues, bat shit, bee stingers, and chicken claws.

I sat at her feet. Not only could she make people fall in love; she also could cure their gout, their acne, their liver disease, and common colds, as well as make them forget bad experiences and have luck with money. She knew how to make people suffer from sharp pain in their private parts and their teeth, and she claimed she even knew how to put them in their graves. "But mind, I never do," she said. She wagged her narrow skull on her skinny neck. "I never kill nobody . . . ." She sucked hard on her pipe, blew out a stinky plume. "Less theys deserve it."

One afternoon, I asked her if she had known my father.

She nodded. "One of the vanished," she said. "They's a passel of 'em."

And she told me people started dropping off the earth early in the century. The first man to own an automobile in Devil's Elbow disappeared in 1910. He cranked up his Ford one day and drove off never to be heard from again. His wife and nine children eventually bundled their belongings and left in a wagon pulled by two horses to live with her sister's family in Cincinnati.

When the second person disappeared, it was 1917 and America was getting into the first world war. The man had just bought a car, and he and the girl he'd been sparking took off on the rattling contraption and vanished into the mist. She was only sixteen—old enough in Devil's Elbow for marriage, for sure, but he was thirty-five, so her parents had been on the fence about the whole deal. The man purchased the car to impress her parents as much as he did to impress the girl. People figured the couple ran off and got married, but nobody ever heard from them again, and the parents would have given in about the marriage anyway, so nobody knew why they wouldn't show back up, maybe with a couple of babies, but they never did, and it led to speculation that they'd been murdered by draft-dodging, German-sympathizing bandits in Portsmouth on the Ohio side of the river and, because they were probably fornicators, sucked into hell by Satan.

More vanished during the 1920s. Then more and more each decade after.

Always vanished without a trace, all friends and family abandoned.

Then again, what was there to stay for in this place, especially if you'd had a fight with your wife or husband or parents or friends? Why stay to work a tobacco patch on the side of a hill year after year as your sole source of money? Grow a few tomatoes? Hope to hook a catfish every once in a while? The only businesses were Mr. Lloyd's gas station-garage-bait-shop and Mr. Davis' general store.

There was an abandoned junk store. There was an abandoned Pentecostal church. There was an abandoned Methodist church.

The FROG church was growing, though.

The Followers and Revelers of God church was housed in an ancient building where beaver pelts were exchanged for flour and whiskey in the eighteenth century. Its members called themselves congregants of the FRG. Everybody else called it the FROG church. The Frogs had special Saturday night services to discourage men from drinking, but everybody knew it just meant the men got started late and then only women and children showed up for the regular Sunday morning services.

Thirteen narrow, crumbling, twisted miles of asphalt separated Devil's Elbow from Pig Gut. Pig Gut was where non-Frogs went to church. It had Baptist, Pentecostal, Church of Christ, and "Non-reformed Methodist" churches. Some of us were nothing and accepted our fate of eternal fire and didn't worry about it.

I was more worried about fuzzy TV reception that skewed the face of Jan Brady on *The Brady Bunch*. Jan was my idea of a pin-up girl. I had even had the fleeting fantasy of making my own love potion based on what Miss Trout had taught me . . . and I'd hitch hike out to Los Angeles—or better, actually get myself a car—and . . . and I'd track down Jan . . . or whatever the name of the actress was . . . . Eve Plumb, I think. My Eve.

Kathy Mayhew reminded me of Jan Brady.

\*\*\*

It was nineteen crumbling, narrow, death-defying asphalt miles to Manchester, a town with a hospital, which was where Mama had a job as a nurse's aide.

Daddy had been the mechanic at Lloyd's Garage. Lloyd's son had worked there too—until he vanished one Saturday night in 1949.

Before the son disappeared, Lloyd was a jolly fat man, Miss Trout told me. She squinted her milky eye and focused her green eye on me. "I tell yo, boy, after Jimbo disappear, Mister Lloyd's heart shrivel up to the size of a acorn. And just as hard. He become a old man overnight."

There were still two old faded signs that Lloyd had hand- painted when he was a jolly fat man: "Lloyd's Is Best Place To Take A Leak" and "Want To Get laid? Crawl up the ~~ass~~ arse of a chicken and wait."

Miss Trout said church people pitched a fit about the word "ass," so Lloyd crossed it out and changed it to what he thought was the polite "arse."

By the mid-1960s so many people had disappeared that Devil's Elbow was infamous along the river. The Frogs believed that Beelzebub had kidnapped Mr. Lloyd's son and all the others who had disappeared.

The Portsmouth, Ohio, newspaper ran a story about Devil's Elbow one Sunday in the late spring of '71. The reporter was Nan Mortimer, a little woman in her forties. She was starting to look dried up and was getting a gray hair here and there. She dressed in the same suit for twenty years that made her look like Lois Lane on the 1950s Superman TV show. Portsmouth wasn't exactly Metropolis, and Nan spent her time running around reporting on fatal stabbings in the bars along the riverfront and the catches of deformed fish and the growing of humungous pumpkins.

The story about Devil's Elbow included a photo of Lloyd's garage sign about taking a leak and included mention of Lloyd's son and my father, as well as a list of all the other mysterious disappearances going back to that first one in 1910.

One elderly interviewee talked about the theory going around in the 1920s that a kind of Loch Ness Monster was snatching cars off the river highway.

Nan Mortimer made a joke about Lloyd's being a good place to take a leak but maybe not such a good place to work, given the two mysterious disappearances. The whole story made Devil's Elbow out to be a joke. The beaten-down, impoverished people of our hamlet grieved for lost loved ones, but the story suggested people just ran off to greener pastures and then further speculated—tongue in cheek—about a connection with the Bermuda Triangle and alien abductions.

Another photo that accompanied the story was of a frowning Gertrude Trout on her porch, giving the camera the evil eye. According to the story, she was known "to whip up a magic potion from time to time to give a friend long life." And there was a picture of me peering through a rusty screen door of what Nan Mortimer described as "Faded Antebellum Gentility." I was trying to see why a woman who looked like Superman's girlfriend was taking a picture of my house. I was a vague figure behind that rusty screen. I looked like a ghost.

At the time of the photo, my sister, Peggy, had been married and gone from home for a year and was living up in Sardinia in Ohio. Mama was at work. Our weedy yard was cluttered with the rusty remnants of my daddy's projects: three engine blocks, two rear axles with wheels, the shell of a 1934 Ford and a front-crushed Lincoln, which had a dark stain on the front seat the shape and size of Texas, and a crumbled, T-boned 1940 Cadillac that was of no use with its bent frame, but I believed it represented a dream my daddy had, an object to keep him focused.

Nan Mortimer wanted a picture of a yard full of old washing machines, ice boxes, chickens, and bony hound dogs, but she had to go down the road for that. We just had the car corpses.

***

The evening of the summer solstice of '71, Peggy moved back in with us, a heart-broken widow.

Her husband, a roofer, had fallen from the peak of the county courthouse up in Hillsboro, Ohio. He looked like a wild boar, or so thought everybody except Peggy, who considered him movie-star

25

handsome. He had landed on his snout. At the funeral, Mama made the snide remark in a low voice to me that it probably improved his looks, although she couldn't say for sure since the casket was closed. People got pleasure back then from being mean like that. Not that human nature has changed for the better. Meanness back then was at least more private, usually whispered from one person to another and often not to the face of the person who would be hurt by it. Nowadays, people get on a computer and display their meanness for the whole world. With all the anti-bullying programs around the country, bullying is worse than ever.

After a week or so, Peggy stopped crying and simply bemoaned the fact that Ronny had been one of the few men around who had all his body parts.

She was right. They missed teeth and fingers mostly. Some missed an arm or, like my father, according to Peggy and Mama, half a leg with a steel peg from the knee down. One man in town had a black patch over an eye. Another had a purple nub where his ear should have been.

Besides missing parts, the men withered away young, or they became inflated with multiple chins, puffed-out cheeks that made their eyes smaller and smaller and bellies that stretched their whiskey-stained flannel shirts. Women didn't fare any better as they staggered toward forty.

# DAY ONE
## *The Preacher*

That spring and summer of 1971, I felt I was on the verge of something. A major change.

*It.*

I was on the verge of *it.*

My instincts were vague and holy, stupid and mysterious, silly and powerful. What I anticipated and what I vaguely feared was somewhat connected with the death of my brother-in-law.

The proximity of death had never been so close. My father had disappeared, but I had no memory of him, and there really was no certainty he was even dead. It was possible he was shacked up with a new wife and kids in Tennessee or Montana. Who knew? It was easy to get lost back then. It was easy to get away with stuff.

Ronnie, though, had lived with us the first six months he and Peggy were married. He and I watched Cincinnati Reds baseball games on TV together. He snuck me his *Playboy*s when he was done caressing the slick pages.

I felt certain with rising fear that at sixteen, if something—*it*—didn't happen soon, I would never quite reach "Manhood," a scary word, like "God." I would become a boy-man instead of a man, and somehow I'd be as good as dead for the rest of my life. I'd be walking around and eating burgers and watching TV and working a lousy job and making lousy money and maybe even fathering some lousy kids, but I'd be almost as dead as Ronnie with his shattered head rotting in the ground.

I tried not to think about it, but I thought about it a lot. When Mama or Peggy caught me staring off into space and asked me what I was thinking about, I said, "Nothin'." And I wasn't exactly lying.

Sixteen years old and one of the worst things about it was I didn't have a car. Part of me felt everything would be fine if I could get a car. But I didn't even have a job except for occasionally helping to harvest a tobacco crop and hanging the leaves in the farmer's barn for curing. When I got those jobs I saved the money. When there was no work on any of the little farms around close by, I'd go to the river and try to catch catfish I could sell at Davis General Store, and Mr. Davis would take a hand-painted wooden sign from behind his counter and lean it outside by the door. The sign said "FRESH CATFISH." He didn't regularly have fresh fish, only when he could buy it as cheap as he bought it from me and early enough in the day people might pick it up for their supper.

I would gather up my fishing pole and rusty tackle box and walk the mile and a half to the Ohio River. The direct route, the descent from the back of our house, was too steep and rugged, so I had to walk narrow Devil's Elbow Road, which wound up and down and around and finally steeply down to join the two-lane highway, Rural Route 6, that ran only two hundred feet from the river all the way up to Maysville.

On July 3rd, I was walking along in the heat so thick I felt like I was pushing through the air with each step into some hazy new world similar to but not quite my own. For some reason, I was wondering about my father on that winding, crumbling rural asphalt. If he had been around, I supposed that he'd be like my friends' fathers, a silent and gaunt figure who smelled of cigarettes and booze and whose infrequent smile revealed small, yellow teeth or no teeth at all.

"Was he tall?" I asked Mama once when I was young enough to care about such things.

"No."

"Peggy says there used to be some old photos."

"Those are long gone."

"Was he short?"

"No."

"Was he skinny?"

"No." She looked out the window, where it was dark and nothing was to be seen except a single dim light in the distant hills. Finally, she said, "He had big feet. . . . A big foot."

I no longer cared that he had named me Cadillac as a promise to love me. That was a little-kid fantasy. I was nearly a grown man now and I knew what I'd seen in the homes of neighbors and my friends. He probably would have used me as slave labor and slapped me around whenever I got on his nerves—or when he just needed something to slap around and nobody else was available. He would have been dumb and cruel, like all the fathers I had observed. He would have had me bringing him beers or moonshine while he sprawled on a moldy sofa. He would have made me or my sister or my mama clean up his puke. He would have had me working odd jobs like shoveling pig shit on some farm and then giving him the money so that he could buy more moonshine.

Mama would be afraid of him. We all would. I told myself I was lucky he had vanished.

I had shed my innocence and my childhood fantasies, for sure. But I had no idea. It turned out he was far worse than my darkest imaginings.

*** 

The sun was blazing so hot on the third of July that the tar of Devil's Elbow Road was sticky by late morning. The road, which was little more than a paved-over wagon trail twisting like a snake, possessed a wicked curve at a point where it actually hung out over the river. Maybe there's a scenic turn-out there now, nearly fifty years later, and tourists park and gaze at the sparkling river and the green hills—I don't know—but in 1971 there was just the curve and not enough ground to anchor a retaining wall. Maybe it hasn't changed. Maybe the road is closed. I don't know. I do know that there's no longer a place called Devil's Elbow. I doubt that anybody much misses it or that many people even remember it.

Until the spring of 1971, I believed that our town got its name from the curve. The road was like an arm bent deeply at the elbow. A bad curve, so why not emphasize its badness, I figured, by calling it the Devil's elbow? A lot of people thought the same thing. I think I even got the idea from Mama.

That spring, though, I was minding my own business in the lunch room at school one day when this kid across the table asked me where I lived. His name was Sanders, and everybody called him "Colonel." Colonel Sanders. He was two years younger than I was, but in my grade, the eleventh because he had been skipped ahead. His father was a veterinarian and his mother was the PTA president, and they lived in Manchester.

I said, "I live in Elbow."

He grinned, revealing a mouth full of shiny braces that cost more than a new car, and said, "Devil's Elbow! Man, you are a *true* hillbilly." He wagged his head, a glare coming off the thick lenses of his glasses. "I bet you don't even know what 'Elbow' really means."

"What 'elbow' means? You think I'm a retard?"

He cackled. A scrawny tow-headed kid. I could have beaten the crap out of him.

"It's a goddamned *euphemism*."

"You what?"

He cackled some more. He even had freckles, so I

didn't understand how he thought he could get away with his bullshit. My faced burned. My hands shook.

"It means '*asshole*,'" he explained with glee. "You live in the Devil's asshole, kid!" Then he noticed how I was glaring at him and figured it was time to leave, so he jumped up and took off across the lunch room, all loose jointed like a rag doll or a scarecrow, still cackling.

***

I got a late start the morning of July 3rd because I'd overslept. My night had been full of wild dreams. Kathy Mayhew had played a starring role in those dreams, and that part was exciting, but Sanders had too, and he actually transfigured into Colonel Sanders with the white suit and goatee and all and kept saying infuriating things like "Finger lickin' good!" And there was a part about the river flooding up all the way to my house. It was like the biblical flood, and it covered the earth, and people and houses and uprooted trees were swept away, and I was carried on the swift current with the bloated corpses of cows, horses, dogs, pigs, and squirrels swirling around me. All around me was darkness— clouds and rain coming down from the sky in sheets, but I was being carried toward a blinding light, like I was being propelled into the very sun. I woke up covered in sweat and with a pounding heart.

Now, with my fishing pole resting on my shoulder, the real sun burned on the back of my neck along with my obsession with the *it* I felt coming. The future burned there—on the back of my neck—and in my feet and in my chest.

And my wild dreams resonated—a mix of excitement, pleasure, and horror.

Off in the distance there was a gunshot. Then another, closer. Somebody shooting squirrels. Or maybe moonshiners gone to war. Then three blasts almost at once from maybe three different guns, before the echoes faded and silence descended.

There was never much traffic. I could walk all the way from my house to the river any time of day and not have a single car or truck pass me from either direction.

I heard the FRG bible-school bus long before it came near. It was an ancient machine and it gave out a distinctive roar. Whenever I heard that low roar— a result of a rusted-out muffler with an undertone of pinging pistons—I stopped to watch it pass. Kathy Mayhew rode that bus.

After a few seconds I knew it was coming too fast.

I could tell from the sound of it, but also I could feel the tremendous force of it bearing down on me.

Then I saw it. It had a long snout and had the old-style head-lamps mounted on the round fenders. It was painted white with "Elbow Church of Followers & Revelers of God" on the side in black block lettering. The Frogs and a lot of others who lived here referred to the town simply as Elbow, leaving off "Devil's," not wanting to acknowledge the Devil's ownership.

I fell back into the shallow ditch as the bus sped past me rocking and weaving on the rough road and smothering me with its hot force. From the ditch, I glimpsed, in one flash of what seemed like a single cell of film, the thin bucktoothed boy who drove the thing. He appeared to be wrestling the steering wheel like it was alive—a writhing animal or a warrior angel. I didn't know his name, but I'd seen him at Davis General Store a couple of times. He was about nineteen. With his mouth closed he looked like church pictures of Jesus, but when he let those bucked teeth slip out, the whole effect was ruined.

There was flash after flash of empty windows. Then a little boy I recognized as Kathy Mayhew's brother. He was in first or second grade. The hair on the back of his head always stuck up like he'd been sleeping on it.

Then in the last window, sitting in the very back of the bus, was Kathy Mayhew with a daisy in her hair. She sat in front of me in English class, and as a result, I never heard a thing Old Iron Maid Johnson ever had to say about *The Red Badge of Courage* or *The Scarlet Letter* or *Animal Farm* because I was always focused on the back of Kathy's neck. Each day she wore either two light-brown braids or just plain pigtails, her hair parted flawlessly in the middle. Growing up in the hills of Kentucky overlooking the river, I had witnessed few straight lines or anything else that was straight—roads, paths, trees, fences. Houses leaned. Cars sat cockeyed.

But it wasn't the perfect straight part in Kathy's hair that fascinated me so much as the perfect white skin of her neck lightly covered in a down of nearly white hair. If she turned and looked at you, you might have expected more perfection, some kind of startling beauty, but that wasn't the case. She had nice full lips and a nice smile that made you feel like she really was glad to see you or really was smiling because she was happy and not smiling just to be faking happiness, like my mama and so many other people I knew, but Kathy was not as pretty as girls on TV, like Jan Brady, or even any of the cheerleaders, and she had perpetually dark circles under her eyes, like she never slept enough.

One lunch hour the past school year, Aesop Duggurt teased Kathy about the circles under her eyes. "You look like one of them zombies. You wanta eat me? Come on, I'll let you eat me."

My face was instantly hot. My head buzzed. I saw dark spots and flashes of lightning. I stood up from the lunch table and I punched him in the mouth, cutting my knuckles on his front teeth.

Then things turned around on me real fast because Aesop was big and dumb and mean and quick as a cat. Before frail old Principal Longing and the football coach could get him off me, he had given me two black eyes and knocked a tooth loose. Afterward, everybody at school let me know I was pretty stupid for going after him. They'd pat my shoulder and say, "You got shit for brains, Cadillac."

In the single flash when I saw Kathy in the last window of that church bus, which picked up the Frog kids early every morning in the summer and then took them home before lunch time, I saw the daisy in her hair better than I did her face. She was facing the front of the bus, and through the open window I heard her screaming. In that instant I saw her, I saw that she was terrified and I saw that she was beautiful.

Maybe because part of my brain was telling me that she was about to be lost to me forever, she looked more beautiful than anything I had ever seen or could imagine.

I still think that about her. And I tell her every day.

Then the bus was past me, smoke flowing from the exhaust pipe in a great purplish plume. The cloud covered me and I choked. Kathy's shrill sixteen-year-old girl's scream melded with the rusted-out muffler and the pinging pistons. And the bus hurled toward disaster.

I squinted down the road, coughing, my eyes watering. It was hard to see the bus through the smoke and my tears, so what happened next was an unreal blur.

The wicked curve was only a few hundred feet away.

The bus's tail lights were the Devil's red eyes peering at me through the smoke and my tears.

The tires never squealed.

Despite the July heat, a cold and perverse thrill

jolted me as the bus seemed to hang in the blue sky a moment, its whiteness shimmering. Part of me expected or hoped to see it float like a balloon or fly like an airplane, maybe even shoot off like a rocket.

Then it dropped nose-first toward the murky river hundreds of feet below.

A second jolt, one of horror, knocked me to my knees, then flat to my face. My fishing gear scattered. The earth reeled. I huffed. Then I was up and running and I had to skid on the heels of my shoes to keep from flying over the edge of the cliff myself. I bowed at the edge, the heels of my shoes on asphalt, the toes hanging in thin air, and I saw the roof of the bus, down the length of which was painted a long black cross. Within seconds, the river boiled up over the cross.

Then there was nothing.

Nothing to see and no sound. The bus' growl, Kathy's screams—gone. Vanished.

And the river flowed on.

I was nodding my head, waiting for whatever came next. Then the birds, which had gone silent as the bus passed, started singing again, but birds singing was not what I was waiting for.

To my right, I heard rustling in the weeds at the

edge of the cliff and turned. He was hunched over dripping blood from his forehead and the palms of his hands, his short-sleeve white button-down-collar shirt torn at the breast, a rip in the knee of one pants leg, out of which protruded a knobby and bloody knee. I stared at him. I didn't know who he was. Then he looked up at me and his eyes seemed as blue as the sky. It was Jesus.

Then he spoke. In tongues, it seemed, because I had no idea what he was saying.

It was the kid who drove the bus.

He mumbled through his buckteeth something I couldn't understand. I stood frozen to the spot where I stood. Blood dripped from his mouth. Then he collapsed like a puppet whose strings had been suddenly released by a careless, bored, or repulsed puppeteer.

Trembling as if the day had turned freezing, I stumbled over to him. I bent and touched his shoulder. I think I said a series of stupid things: "You okay? Stay here. I'll get help. Everything will be okay. What's your name? It's not your fault."

I stood up straight and looked at the sun, the sky, the river. Of the next several minutes, I remember only the slap of my sneakers on the asphalt, the rasp of my breathing, the thundering of my heart, my mind whirling with a rehearsal of the words I would use to describe the horror of what I had witnessed.

*** 

Miss Trout had said Lloyd used to be a jolly fat man. Now he was small, and folds of skin sagged from his face and arms. He stabbed me with his old man eyes. I couldn't catch my breath. My leg muscles had given out and I had staggered up to his gas station like I was sick on bad moonshine (a lot of men were blind because of bad liquor) or like I was having a bad LSD trip (a boy at my school had dropped dead the year before).

Mr. Lloyd was pumping gas into a stranger's shiny black Buick Riviera, a fine expensive car. The stranger, a white-haired man in a black suit, was standing by him, arguing, completely ignoring me.

"You can't say that. You can't say that, my friend!" the stranger was saying. "You have no right. I have dedicated my life to showing my flock the path of righteousness."

Mr. Lloyd was known for insulting everybody he had contact with. Some sweet-looking old lady would pull up to his garage and say, "Beautiful day," and he would respond with a long stream of nasty brown tobacco spit and, "You can go straight to hell, you old bitch."

He turned to the stranger and spewed a string of obscenities, took a breath, and then said, "Path to your pockets, Mr. Preacher Man. You drivin' a new Buick . . . a Buick *Riviera*, for Christ's sake . . . but how many of your flock is? Flock of chickens they is. Stupid as chickens."

"You surely believe in our lord, my friend. None enter His kingdom but by His way. Surely, my friend, you know of *The Way!*"

I was still working my mouth hopelessly. My throat was raw. Sweat stung my eyes, but my perception was intense. Details sharper. Colors brighter. The little red veins in Mr. Lloyd's nose. The purple mole behind his left jaw.

The Preacher's face was deeply lined, his dark eyes intense and distressed, his hair white as whole milk. A green vein throbbed violently in his liver-spotted forehead. His liver-spotted hands waved as he spouted a few bible verses I only vaguely recognized from before Mama gave up on God.

Mr. Lloyd hung the gas nozzle back on the pump and spit again. "Ain't no God. Ain't nothin' but misery."

The Preacher spread his arms wide. "The Lord saves and protects! Mark my words, friend, there is a God and there is a Devil."

"Then the Devil reigns."

A wail came out of my mouth, long and high-pitched, and I spun around, clutching my head.

The Preacher finally looked at me and said, "This boy retarded? . . . Poor thing."

I blew out a breath and then I was almost all right. "The church bus went over the cliff. Into the . . . the river."

They gawked at me. Mr. Lloyd said, "Say that again."

"The bible bus. Frog . . . bus." My lungs and my throat burned.

The Preacher said, "From the F.R.G. bible school? I just came from there!"

"It went over the cliff. At that big curve . . . hangs over the river."

Mr. Lloyd's eyes got big. "Jesus Christ!"

"The driver jumped out, I guess, 'cause he's layin' in the weeds at the edge of the cliff. He's all banged up. He looks bad. Blood . . . Blood . . . " I felt dizzy and realized that I hadn't been breathing. I took in deep breaths. Mr. Lloyd and The Preacher stood frozen.

"This not some prank?" Mr. Lloyd said. "This ain't like that radio show with Martians or somethin'?"

I flung my arms up like I was going to take flight. "Goddamn it! I watched the bus sink."

"Jesus Christ," he said again.

The Preacher looked at an oil stain on the asphalt. "I just blessed those children."

Mr. Lloyd gave The Preacher a fierce look. "A lot of good it did 'em."

"Call for help!" I said. "We got to get them out."

Then Mr. Lloyd turned his fierce look onto me. "Get them out? They're all dead, boy. I can guarantee you that."

"But . . . but . . .. What about the driver?"

Mr. Lloyd gave a jerk, nodded, turned, and hustled into the office of his garage. Through the fly-speckled glass, I saw him on the phone. The Preacher was running his gnarly old fingers over his face and head like he was trying to grasp something and looking off in the direction of the river. His eyes were shiny.

When Mr. Lloyd came outside, he said, "They're comin'. Life squad from Manchester. Get in my truck." The Preacher and I both got into Mr. Lloyd's '39 Studebaker pick-up. "Show me."

"Down . . . Devil's Elbow Road. That big curve. You know!"

Mr. Lloyd's pick-up roared down the winding, tree-lined road at a speed that terrified me, passing through alternating patches of bright sunlight and deep shadow. My fishing pole lay in the middle of the road, and the truck tires shattered it into kindling.

We stopped at the height of the curve. There was no place to pull over, and I jumped out and ran into the weeds where I had left the bus driver. He had turned over onto his back. His arms were spread wide, and he stared wide-eyed straight into the noon sun. The Preacher came up and took his black hat off and started muttering a prayer.

Mr. Lloyd said, "Perkins boy. This will kill his ma and pa."

Then he turned, dropped to his knees, and sobbed.

I stepped over to the edge of the cliff and looked down. The river sparkled in the sun. In the distance, a tugboat moved toward Cincinnati. There was no sign of the bus. The river had swallowed it whole.

***

Mr. Lloyd sobbed on his knees, his shoulders shaking, for what seemed a long time. The tall, lean

Preacher stood over the dead boy, muttering prayers. I didn't know what to do. It seemed somebody ought to do something worthwhile. Crying and praying seemed a waste of time. I kept thinking I should go down to the river bank, but I didn't know what I would do there. I could jump in and swim over to where the bus went in. But the river was deep, and I probably wouldn't be able to hold my breath long enough to swim down to the bus.

I wandered back and forth between Mr. Lloyd and the edge of the cliff. As I stood at the edge, the asphalt started crumbling under my feet. I imagined it crumbling completely away and me dropping to the river, and for a second I didn't care... Then I stepped back.

I heard a siren that was faint at first but quickly got louder.

When I turned back toward Mr. Lloyd again, he was struggling up off his knees. On his feet, he swayed. Then without a glance toward me or The Preacher he hurried to his pick-up, climbed in, fired the ignition, and took off like a bat out of hell back in the direction of his garage. He almost ran head-on into the life squad coming our way. He swerved over just in time, but didn't slow down.

The life squad pulled up, its siren off now but its red bubble light still turning and shining. The driver got out. "Crazy bastard! Who was that? I'll report him."

Another man got out on the other side, and they hurried over to the bus driver, but as soon as they saw him, they both froze and said, "Ah, hell."

The Preacher looked at me. "Let's walk down, boy. See what we can do at the river."

I'm sure the look I gave him was one of amazement. *See what we can do.* Was he serious? In a few minutes I had gone from believing someone needed to take positive action to accepting that all was lost. Any action would be a waste of energy. The bus was gone. Kathy Mayhew was dead.

The Preacher was drenched in sweat, and his face was bright pink. His wrinkles had turned from dry creek beds into flowing streams.

*See what we can do.*

I nodded, and we started walking. I looked over my shoulder and saw the ambulance men pulling a stretcher out of the back of the life squad. They were taking their time.

We ambled down the middle of the road. No cars or trucks came along. The road bubbled like a pan of grease from the fierce sun. Waves of heat distorted the world.

Near the bottom of the hill, we came to the Mayhews' house. It was a small clapboard house with dark-green paint flaking off to reveal an old coat of yellow. The Preacher was a stranger and didn't know it was the house of people who had just lost their only two children. I felt no inclination to tell him.

A stout woman in a long gray dress—the uniform of Frog women—and with her hair pulled into a tight bun came out onto the porch and looked up and down the road. She gripped the porch rail and looked worried. She didn't acknowledge me or The Preacher as we walked by.

By the time we got to the river bank, a long black Cadillac hearse with tailfins like a jet plane was there parked beside two Kentucky Highway Patrol cruisers, big Ford Custom 500s, on the side of the road next to the Rural Route 6 concrete retaining wall. The hearse had "Manchester Funeral Home" painted along the back in fancy gold letters. Manchester had everything, people said—a funeral home, a veterinary clinic, and even a Catholic church.

The wall ended at a clump of trees. The Preacher

and I pushed through the trees and came out on the river bank. A tall, skinny man and a short fat man (like Abbot and Costello), both in white dress shirts and black trousers, stood with their arms folded, talking to the troopers.

The Preacher and I walked up to the four men, and one of the troopers was saying, "All I know is we got this call but I don't see anything."

The fat man frowned like he was disappointed. "You think it's a prank?"

The Preacher said, "There's a dead boy up on the ridge. He was the one driving the bus. Jumped out just before the bus went over."

The four men all looked at him.

"This boy here saw the bus go over."

And they all frowned at me and looked me up and down like I was responsible somehow. I looked out at the river and saw something floating toward shore.

It was a daisy.

***

Just around the time the daisy drifted to the muddy bank and I reached down and picked it up, Kathy and Kent Mayhew's worried mother called the FRG church. It was a little after noon. The Frog preacher,

Mr. John Black, told Mrs. Mayhew that he didn't know why her children weren't home from morning bible school, that no one else had called, that the bus must have broken down before its last stop, which was the Mayhews' house. He added that Kent and Kathy, along with the other FRG children, had been spiritually stirred by a guest preacher from West Virginia, a man who spoke in tongues daily and had handled many a snake and rabid rat over the seventy-five years of his life and never been bitten. This man had once descended into a pit of voracious rats, and the rodents had swarmed all over him, but not a one even nipped him.

Mrs. Mayhew, who was growing impatient with the longwinded Mr. Black, finally exploded: "I don't give a rat's ass! I want to know where my children are!"

How do I know all this?

I don't know. Maybe I imagined it or read about it or a combination. Maybe I just now, fifty years later, made it up, but I'm sure of its general truth, if not the accuracy of every detail.

I stared at the daisy—Kathy's daisy—lying in the palm of my hand for I don't know how long. The sun beat down, and my head throbbed. My hands were dirty, and for the first time I noticed that there was blood on the tips of my fingers. The blood must have been the bus driver's. I had touched him and talked to him, and now he was dead. I had barely said two words to Kathy the whole time I knew her. I had certainly never touched her. And now she was . . . gone.

I thought the word "gone" because it was easier than the finality of "dead." People who were "gone" might come back.

I was starting to lose track of time. The world had leaped ahead a few minutes without me. Later, it would take leaps of hours, leaving me behind in my funk to catch up later.

When I looked up, The Preacher, still wearing his black suit, was standing in the river up to his waist. One of the troopers shouted to him that he should get out, but the other trooper said to let him be. "Crazy old coot. Who cares?"

Abbot and Costello from the funeral home were gone, probably deciding to wait at the Big Boy Burger Drive-In or Pig Patty's in Manchester until they had some cargo to haul.

The Preacher had his arms spread, palms up, and his face lifted to the merciless sun. He hollered,

"Undo this work of Satan. Undo the Devil's mischief. Shift the earth and time to mock Mephistopheles!"

Two more state troopers showed up. The way the sun reflected off their polished leather boots hurt my eyes. I heard them tell the first ones that divers were coming. One of them pointed at The Preacher and asked what he was doing.

"Bible thumper," one of the first troopers said.

The Preacher kept talking to the sun.

A speed boat raced toward us from a distance, the motor whining high; then it cut off and the boat drifted in to shore. One of the troopers pointed at me and said, "That boy says he saw it."

The guy in the boat wore a uniform and a cap with a star on the front. He shook his head. All the men watched The Preacher for a moment. The man in the cap said, "Crazy coot."

Then all five men walked back to the road and I heard their car doors slam and the big Ford engines roar, and I was alone on the river bank with The Preacher out in the water. I looked back at the daisy in my hand, and I discovered that I had crushed it.

As the sun moved and dropped, The Preacher shifted his position, and his profile became a rainbow-colored silhouette against the sun, and the sun's rays behind him seemed to radiate from him, as though the pores of his skin and the fabric of his suit shot forth beams of light.

"Undo the horrors of the day, oh Lord, or the Devil dances with glee!" The Preacher stood rigid, only his jaw moving. Sweat poured from his face, the redness of it deepening, all of him radiant with the spectrum of the rainbow, but he mostly seemed golden.

***

Time took another leap, and unaware that the troopers had returned, I found one standing close to me and studying my face, his head cocked, his eyes squinted, sweat on his cheeks glistening. Then he looked out to The Preacher.

"What you got there, boy?" he asked, still looking at The Preacher.

"Got?"

"In your hand."

"Oh. Nothin'." I opened my hand. He looked at me again, and I showed him the mashed daisy.

He nodded at it, then looked back to The Preacher. "How old are you?"

"Sixteen."

"Really?"

"Yes, sir."

"Sixteen?"

I swallowed. I didn't say anything.

"You saw that bus go in the water from up there?" He jerked his long chin at the cliff, and he looked at me, and I looked out at the river glittering by.

"Yeah."

"You see why it went over?"

I shook my head slowly. "It was going too fast. I think the brakes went out. I don't know." My voice was a flat echo in my head, like somebody else from a distance was talking.

"Animal jump out in front of it? Raccoon? Deer maybe?"

"I didn't see any animals. It just flew off the cliff. Maybe the gas pedal got stuck." I wondered why it mattered but didn't ask.

"Were you walking in the road, boy?"

"Yes."

"How did you get out of the way?"

"I fell in the ditch."

He nodded. "You know that man out there in the water?"

"He's a preacher."

"He your preacher?"

"No. He was visiting the Frog bible camp."

"*What kind* of bible camp?"

"It's a church here in Elbow. Frogs. FRG Church. I forget what the letters really stand for."

He nodded. Then he asked me my full name and my parents' names and where I lived and what my phone number was, and he wrote it all down in a little notebook with a stubby yellow pencil that had teeth marks in it and a worn-down eraser.

"What happens now?" I asked.

"To you?"

"The bus. The people."

"Divers will pull 'em out. If they can."

The trooper walked away. He wore high black boots and his gray pants had a black stripe down them. He wore a wide black holster that held a pistol. His shoulders were broad. He had dark stubble on his chin. People would say he was a "*real* man." In that moment, I felt that what I was going through would not propel me into manhood. Instead, I felt beaten and stifled. I wanted to cry and be with my mama. I felt I was always going to be a boy.

\*\*\*

Time took a short leap. I don't know how I got there or why I went there, but I found myself sitting on the river bank next to a small dump site. A frog jumped. A turtle slid into the water. Mosquitoes and jiggers buzzed in clouds. A dead-fish stench wafted from the water on the first breeze I'd felt all day. Then the breeze died, and the sun kept blaring down. A cottonmouth slithered past me. The Preacher stood stock still in the river, only his jaw moving. "I will not abide, Lord! The Devil shall not win this day!"

Time jumped again. Or disappeared down a hole the way it does sometimes. It just disappears and you can't find it when you go back to look. Maybe I fell asleep sitting there.

The Preacher was still in the water when the two divers showed up. They came through the clump of trees that separated River Route 6 from the river bank, carrying their air tanks, wet suits, masks, and fins. As they put on their gear, people who lived nearby started showing up curious about what was going on. The troopers told them that *allegedly* a church bus had gone into the river.

Some of the people ran off to tell others.

The men from the funeral home came back. They carried folded body bags in one hand and a Styrofoam cup with a straw in the other, *Big Boy* printed around the cup. They stood around sucking on their straws until they got nothing but air and then tossed the cups on the ground. There was already lots of trash on the river bank, especially where I sat: a pile of worn-out or blown-out car and truck tires and a couple of lawnmower carcasses and washing machines and a refrigerator.

The refrigerator door was closed, and suddenly, I felt terror of what might be inside—maybe a man's head or a little dead kid. I looked away and pushed the thought from my mind.

For a moment, a small shiny red propeller plane buzzed overhead.

The divers got in the boat with the man wearing the starred cap, and the boat started, and The Preacher hollered above the high-pitched whine of the boat motor, waving his arms.

The boat went out to the spot below the cliff, and the motor cut off. The Preacher was now whirling his arms in circles and his head vibrated crazily—like somebody holding a high-voltage wire. He got croaky and whispery like he was losing his voice, but then, all of a sudden, loud gibberish issued from his lips. The language of God, I supposed. I'd never seen a Frog or even a Pentecostal in action. When the divers splashed and disappeared into the water from the boat, The Preacher was still twirling his arms and talking his wild nonsense. One of the divers came up out of the water and gave the guy in the boat a thumbs-up, then disappeared again.

A siren sounded in the distance and grew louder and louder. The sun had turned yellow as a hound dog's piss. The red airplane was gone.

A muffled sound of rending steel sounded from the river out where the divers and the boat were, and the water boiled up like in a cauldron, large bubbles bursting on the surface. The boat rocked violently, and the man with the starred cap, who had been standing in it, fell down. I could see only the top of his cap, and he stayed down while the boat kept rocking.

The Preacher fell backwards into the water—so cleanly there was hardly a splash—and disappeared. I jumped up, waiting for him to reappear, holding my breath. Finally, my lungs were about to burst, and I hollered, "Help him!" I turned toward two troopers and yelled, "The Preacher went under." They were staring out at the commotion around the boat, and I had to holler again. Finally, they waded out into the water, and before they got far, The Preacher floated up, his arms and legs spread, his face gray in the bright sunlight.

Each trooper took an arm and they pulled him in. They stumbled up onto the bank, dragging him up onto a little incline. They stood a few seconds, breathing hard. Then one of the troopers placed two fingers against the big vein in The Preacher's neck. He held it there, looking off at the woods, then shook his head. The other trooper was already pressing on The Preacher's chest. Three compressions, then mouth to mouth. Three compressions, blow. The Preacher's face was slack, most of his wrinkles gone. Three more compressions, three more breaths.

The trooper's efforts went on for a couple of minutes. The siren was close now out on the road. Then the siren cut out, and a few seconds later, another trooper walked out of the trees onto the bank.

Another siren started wailing. It came from the boat, which rocked only a little now. The man standing in it was shaking his head and yelling, "Get help!"

The river out by the boat had stopped boiling. The water looked smooth. The trooper trying to revive The Preacher looked around, spat.

The two divers were nowhere in sight.

On the river bank, The Preacher's head sagged

sideways, his face toward me like he was looking at me, but his eyes were closed.

A woman's wail came out of the trees that separated the highway from the river bank. Then the woman appeared, her hair crazy, her eyes crazy, her face twisted in agony, screaming, "Where's my babies? Where's my babies?"

It was Mrs. Mayhew.

I looked at The Preacher's gray face. His white hair was plastered wet to his head. His face was so smooth he looked like a baby with white hair.

Kathy's mama's face was red as boiled crawfish. Tears glistened on her cheeks like tiny diamonds.

She stumbled into the river a few yards, then fell, and was gone. The trooper who had taken The Preacher's pulse went in after her and she fought him off. She clubbed his head with her fists and slashed his face and neck with her fingernails. The trooper who had been pumping The Preacher's chest went in after her too, and after what seemed a long time, the two troopers dragged her out and flung her on the bank next to The Preacher, and she screamed and screamed, shaking her head furiously, and her hair, which had come all undone, whipped back and forth across her face. Her dress was ripped wide open and her heavy breasts sagged naked and white and bobbed as her shoulders heaved.

One of the troopers said, "It's going to be all right, ma'am."

She cursed him and wailed, "My babies!"

He approached her, and she kicked straight up. He dropped to his knees, holding his privates.

Her hands opened and closed. "Let me die!" she screamed. "Let me die!"

The trooper glared at her with such rage I thought he'd pull his revolver and blow her brains out.

Her head continued to swivel back and forth until her eyes latched onto me. "Boy!" she hollered at me. "My babies are in there! Go save them! Go! Hurry! Please!"

Then time took a leap for me again. Or escaped down a snake hole there on the banks of the Ohio River, July 3rd, 1971.

***

In the early evening with about three hours of light left, two new divers went down to fish out the bodies of the first divers, as well as Kathy and her brother. They stayed down a long time, and everybody frowned, their faces taut, sweaty, red. Some people shook their heads slowly. Some prayed.

All of us on the river bank watched the placid water intently. The troopers and funeral-home men gave each other tense glances. A new trooper, an older man with some gray hair and three stars on his shoulders, pulled a cigar out of his breast pocket and started chewing it.

Finally, the divers surfaced, and everybody let out a sigh. One held a rectangle of metal in his hand. Otherwise, they had surfaced with nothing.

When they were back on shore, they quickly, jerkily shrugged off their oxygen tanks and, still in their wet suits and flippers, lifted off their masks and dropped them on the dried mud and they started talking excitedly to the older trooper, who started shouting: "What? Say that *again*."

I left my pile of tires and other trash and got closer.

One of the divers was slim and blond and boyish. He waved his arms around. He said, "The bus shifted. It's on its side and all cockeyed on top of . . . of this pile . . . . A pile . . . a whole damned *mountain* of cars and trucks. Maybe twenty. Maybe thirty. Some look real old, been down there for maybe forty or fifty years."

I moved up right next to them. I looked from one

amazed face to another. They paid me no mind. I could have been a ghost.

The trooper said to the other diver, "This what you saw too?"

The other diver, who was young too but dark-haired, just kept staring out at the river. He didn't say anything but he held up what he had in his hand: a rusty license plate dated 1923.

*\*\**

After she got home from work, Mama came looking for me, wearing her nurse-aide uniform. Word had gotten around. Neighbor told neighbor. Phone calls were made. Drivers on the country roads waved each other down to tell the news. All kinds of people had gathered on the river bank—old people, young moms with little kids, teenagers, men coming from their jobs. Even moonshiners, who had no phones, had heard somehow and came down from their mountain hideouts to see what was going on. The Moonshiners had straggly beards and long hair like hippies.

Word was out about all those vehicles in the river. Some people said there were twenty, some said fifty, some said there were hundreds. And everybody said, *You think they've got people in them?*

Already, everybody was thinking and talking

about all the vanishings since early in the century.

Mama had heard what I'd been through, so when she came up to my pile of worn-out and blown tires on the river bank, she sat down next to me, put her arm around my shoulders, and kissed my cheek. "Hi, Cadillac," she said.

"Hi, Mama," I whispered, and my chin quivered. I let her hug me, and then I let myself cry into her shoulder.

All kinds of emotions swelled up from my gut and chest, and they spilled out of me in a torrent of tears. I didn't care if the others on the river bank saw me and thought I was a sissy.

It was a long storm.

When I was able to stop, Mama and I just sat shoulder to shoulder, me leaning limp against her, and I felt her looking at me for a while, and then she and I both watched the approach of a barge with a crane standing on it. It had been five miles upriver at the construction site of a new bridge. For a good year, people had been talking about how that bridge was going to change lives in the vicinity of Devil's Elbow. The bridge would bring tourists and businesses and cross-country eighteen-wheelers, and there'd have to be a big truck stop with a dozen fuel pumps and a diner and showers for the truckers and a big-rig truck wash, and some clean and decent-looking prostitutes.

The crane was amazingly big and seemed almost like a mechanical monster as it neared, maybe a giant robot out of a Japanese sci-fi movie, maybe a steel god looming over everything.

Mama hadn't said anything for a long while and her voice startled me: "Folks are saying all the disappearances we've had round here all these years are about to be explained real soon." She nodded at the crane.

I was slow, but after a minute, I said, "Like my father."

"Yes, like your daddy."

We fell silent again.

The sun was setting.

By the time the barge got positioned, stars were starting to appear and the horizon was red and gold. The dredging would start in the morning. People began ambling back to the river road.

Mama said softly, "Let's go home, Cad baby."

I shrugged, then shook my head slowly. "You go on. I'll come in a bit."

"Why?"

"I just . . . I don't know . . . "

"You sure?" She put her hand on my boney shoulder.

"Yeah."

She looked at me a long time before she nodded and walked away in her white nurse-aide shoes.

I stood and looked down at the brown river lapping at my feet. The crushed daisy was in my jean's left front pocket, the pocket I kept money in whenever I had a little money. I kept my Swiss Army knife that had belonged to my father in my right-hand pocket. I took the daisy out. It was falling apart and I told myself I didn't want to keep it, to watch it shrivel up and dry out, so I dropped it. It just lay there on the water until it decided to float up against my foot.

A pressure built in my head and face, and I shook my head hard like I would to shoo off a fly or a wasp, and I looked out at the blinding red setting sun, and then I sat down and lay back on a tractor tire, and I stopped thinking about anything—not Kathy or her brother or the bus driver or The Preacher or the first two divers. . . .

Time flew away like a little bird spooked by a hawk.

\*\*\*

When I woke up, I opened my eyes to shimmering stars in a black sky and a full moon. I heard rustling sounds in the grass and the rippling of the river. Then my heart was suddenly pounding, and I was scared, and I thought about ghosts. If there were such a thing as ghosts, I didn't want to see them.

But first, I needed to open that old refrigerator lying there cockeyed on the dump heap. Whatever it contained was probably far worse than any ghost, but I just couldn't walk away without knowing what that refrigerator held. I'd been glancing at it all day, and now it glistened in the moonlight, securely shut. As I stared at it now, all the noises of the river—the rustlings in the grass, the rippling of the water, the chirping of crickets, the songs of locusts—seemed to come from inside of that old ice box.

My legs trembled as I stepped close to it. My hand shook as it reached for the chrome-plated handle. When I pulled the handle, it lifted loosely and silently. It was broken. I let go of it and it fell limply, like something dead.

I stepped back, relieved for a moment that the thing was still shut. I could walk away now, I told myself, but before I took a single step toward the river road, I lunged toward the rusty old machine in a fit of passion—of hunger for knowing—and grasped the edge of its door with both hands and heaved.

There was a loud sucking sound, an explosion of ancient air released; the door flew back at me; and I fell backwards into a heap of old milk cartons and disposable diapers. I lay there a while, sweating, my lungs aching, my heart pounding.

Time was not a rabbit leaping down holes. It was a tortoise ambling across my belly.

I stood, slowly leaned to see the inside of the refrigerator.

Dozens of dead rats.

A rotting raccoon.

A rotted human head.

A little dead kid.

Nothing.

It was empty. A void. Still, as I stood there shivering and blinking in the hot night, I felt that void waiting to be filled with some unspeakable horror.

***

On my entire walk home, not a single car passed me on Devil's Elbow Road. A pack of seven or eight hound dogs did pass, all heading down to the river. They weren't running or trotting but just ambling along. They glanced at me with indifference, too old or too hot to care.

Although the sun had long been down, the road still held the heat of the day. It burned through the soles of my cheap shoes.

Kathy Mayhew's house was all lit up, and at least a dozen cars—all old beaters—were parked around the side and front. It had to be crowded inside, but not a sound came from the house. All those people, and they had been struck dumb, I figured. Why talk? What could be said? There was no explanation for the events of the day. No one was praying. No one was singing hymns. No one was speaking in tongues.

I walked on.

An owl hooted. In the moonlight I saw my shattered fishing pole lying in the road. I kicked a splintered piece of it off into the ditch. A dog howled in the distance. Somebody fired a shotgun not too far away, and I instinctively ducked my head and walked faster.

I was winded when I got to the top of the hill where our old house stood black against the deep-blue-black of the star-filled sky. One light was on, in the back in the kitchen.

Mama was waiting up in the dark front parlor. I saw her through the screen window as I crossed the yard. She was bathed in the gray light of the black-and-white TV. We could get three channels on that old Zenith. Every house, shack, and trailer home around Devil's Elbow had a tall aluminum aerial on its roof in order to get those three channels, one from Huntington, West Virginia, and two from Cincinnati. I came in and sat down next to Mama on the sofa. She was watching the eleven o'clock news.

The weather man said the holiday was going to set a record high temperature. "We have never seen heat like this," he said, "and there will not be a cloud in the sky. You probably want to stay in the pool or head out to a lake or the river and stay in the water all day." The weather man grinned like crazy.

Then the camera turned to the anchorman, who looked as somber as somebody at a funeral and announced that the federal government was predicting 600 deaths on the nation's highways over the holiday weekend.

"You hear that?" Mama said. "I don't think I want you ever driving."

I shrugged. "Have to. I'm sixteen."

She reached over and pulled me against her. "You don't *have* to." I felt her staring at me the way she often did. "My goodness, why did you have to grow up?"

I shrugged. I wasn't sure I had.

A beer commercial came on. A big mug foamed and spilled over. Mama had my head smashed against her shoulder. She smelled like the hospital—soap and bleach. I wondered how many dead people she saw in a month. Or a week. Or a day. I had never asked her.

I said, "If I didn't grow up, I'd be dead."

She squeezed me even harder. "Don't you say such things." Then she let me go and kept looking at me.

The TV said there was a sale on all new Dodges, Chryslers, and Plymouths the entire Independence Day weekend. Mama pulled away a little and said, "I don't have to work tomorrow. I'm going down to the river in the morning to see . . . Well, just to see."

"I'm going too."

"You sure? You sure you're okay? You been through a lot, honey."

"I want to see too."

***

Moonlight shined through my window, and my room was alive with shadows. Despite my nap on the river bank, I was exhausted, but when I closed my eyes I saw things I didn't want to see, so I couldn't sleep. I also saw things with my eyes open, so I tried staring out the window at the moon, but it started looking like a skull, so I turned over onto my stomach and pressed my face into my pillow.

I had to lie in a certain spot on my old mattress or I got poked by springs. Mama often said that a new mattress for my bed was one thing she absolutely had to buy when she got a little ahead on bills (she had a car payment on her Mercury Comet, and the gas and electric bills were always high in our big old house, and groceries weren't free, and there were her uniforms and shoes, and my school clothes . . .

I hadn't seen my sister, Peggy, after I got home, but I heard her radio through the wall as I drifted between consciousness and sleep. Ever since Ronnie died, she couldn't sleep without leaving the radio on all night. Tonight, she had the radio turned up louder than usual, and the disc jockey spun back-to-back Doors songs: "Light My Fire," "L.A. Woman," "Riders on the Storm." A kaleidoscope of colors—a kind of psychedelic light show—played on the backs of my eyelids. It was a lot better than what I had been seeing.

Then the volume of the music went low, and the DJ talked over it. "The Lizard King, Mr. Mojo Risin,

Jim Morrison . . . dead. Today. July Third, 1971, in Paris, France. He was twenty-seven years old." Then the music got loud again.

My eyes popped open to the blackness of the room, to nothingness.

Jimi Hendrix had died the year before. Janice Joplin too.

You didn't have to be old, like The Preacher, to die.

And I thought about the kid who drove the church bus. I wished I could get those wide eyes staring at the sun out of my head and those buck teeth.

People died at any age, all ages. Sooner or later, people died. Mama wished I'd never grown up. But like I told her . . .

Then it hit me that time was a horrible thing. Maybe I was drifting back off to sleep by this point, "Love Her Madly" playing through the wall from Peggy's radio. Of all the horrors of life I was aware of at the age of sixteen, it had never occurred to me how awful time was. Even Miss Trout would die. Time would catch her yet. Even if she was a witch. I wondered what she had looked like fifty years ago. Sixty. Eighty. Ninety years ago, when she was a kid. *Now look at her. Look at what time has done to her.*

All kinds of things could catch you—a bullet, a

knife, a slick road, a hair-pin curve, a log truck, a drunk driver, faulty wiring, a lightning strike, a thrown rock, a falling brick, an icy step . . . Countless things *could* get you. Time was the one thing that got you *for sure*. There was no escape from time by the skin of your teeth. There simply was no escape.

Mama was always saying "forever." *You'll remember this forever. You'll be this way forever. You'll regret this forever. I'll love you forever*. It was all a lie. Only death was forever.

"The End" was in the middle of playing.

I dreamed of hot black asphalt. I dreamed of an albino frog sailing across a red sky. I dreamed of The Preacher standing in the river, his old flesh sunburned and sagging, and he was singing "Love Her Madly" in Jim Morrison's voice. Then Kathy was the one standing in the river, not The Preacher, and she looked over her shoulder at me standing on the bank—I looked like I was three years old with a baby face but I had white hair—and she said to me softly, "Forever." And a gigantic crushed daisy the size of a tug boat floated on the water until it morphed into a rainbow that started at my feet and disappeared far in the distance, into blinding light.

# DAY TWO
## *The Dead*

The next morning, Mama was up by four-thirty. Actually, I wasn't sure she'd ever gone to bed. She was scrambling eggs and flipping pancakes with a manic energy I rarely saw, except when she was excited about something (like a ten-cent raise at work) or when she was pissed off about something (like the time she came home early from work because she had the flu and caught Peggy half naked with some boy). Usually, we all had cold cereal— Corn Flakes or Wheaties without sugar and with skim milk. She got out the old and seldom-used coffee percolator instead of making instant coffee or re-using a day-old tea bag to make weak stuff that barely tasted like more than hot water. The house was full of the aroma of fresh-brewed coffee, a smell I associated with Christmas and Easter mornings. It was so strong it largely masked the usual smells of grease and cigarettes and mold. Since she wasn't going to work, she didn't put on her olive-green uniform and white sneakers. Instead, weirdly, she put on heels and a white dress she hadn't worn in years, not since she had dragged me and Peggy to the Baptist church in Pig Gut.

Mama drove very slowly down Devil's Elbow Road toward the river. Biting her lower lip, Mama took the hairpin turn with her foot on the brake. From the passenger seat I saw no road or ground beneath us, only a sheer drop to the river.

Peggy was with us, even though at six in the morning she had to wake up six hours earlier than usual for her. She hadn't worked when she was married to Ronnie because he made good money doing the roofing, and they figured she'd be having babies quick enough. Now Mama kept telling her she needed to go to the junior college in Portsmouth and become a nurse aide or take culinary classes so she could be a cook in a restaurant, but Peggy claimed she was too blue yet to go on with her life. On this morning, Mama dragged Peggy's butt out of bed and told her we were going to make it a family day. My sister moaned and groaned and fell asleep in the backseat of Mama's orange Mercury Comet.

I said, "I think Peggy stayed up all night listening to Jim Morrison songs."

"Who?"

"You know, The Doors. Jim Morrison died yesterday."

Mama nodded. "Drugs probably. I better never catch you doin' drugs."

"I think Peggy was upset about Jim Morrison."

"Now when Hank Williams died, *that* was sad."

As we descended the last stretch of Devil's Elbow Road, Mama said, "Big day. Yes, sir, a big day."

I didn't understand how she could sound or be so happy, but later I realized that she was anticipating answers—she was going to find out, she hoped, that her husband hadn't abandoned us at all. He had gone flying off that cliff. Not his fault. More importantly, not her fault, either.

Then she said, "We should have a picnic. Would you like that?"

But I didn't answer because we had just arrived at the bottom of the road where the Mayhews lived. All the cars from the night before were gone except for the Mayhews' Ford station wagon. In place of those cars of concerned neighbors, friends, and church folk were three state trooper cars, the county sheriff's car, and two dusty black hearses pulled up in the yard right next to the porch.

The Mayhews' closest neighbors, the Adamses, were standing in the road. The three Adams kids were all tow-headed. Their mama was a red head. Their daddy was blond as Marilyn Monroe. Mama pulled up to them. Her window was already rolled down, and Mrs. Adams said without waiting to be asked, "Albert heard shotgun blasts and went over to see what they'd shot, and when he went in—" She didn't finish. Her eyes were stretched wide and were red from crying. She covered her mouth to stifle a sob and turned away. Mr. Adams was in the yard of the Mayhews' house talking to a trooper.

Abbot and Costello from the Manchester funeral home came out the front door of the house with a stretcher. A white sheet covered a body and was blood soaked where the body's torso was. They took the body to one of the hearses. Then two more funeral-home men came out with a second body covered by a sheet, and the blood soaking through was where the head was.

Mama shivered. "Lord. Oh, my lord. He shot her and then himself?"

Mrs. Adams shook her red curls furiously and turned back to Mama's window. She blurted, "No!"

"No? Then what—?"

"*She* shot *him*. In the chest. Then she put the shotgun in her mouth. . . . Or that's what Albert figures."

"Oh, good lord."

I stuck my head out the passenger window and puked up my entire breakfast. The best breakfast I'd had in months.

Mama was pale now and deflated. "Oh, honey, you wanta go home?" Mama said to me.

I shook my head. "No. I wanta do this. It's a big day, you said."

Peggy slept through it all. Just as well.

\*\*\*

Because a lot of cars and pickup trucks and even a couple of farm tractors were already there, we had to park far down the river wall from the opening to the river bank. We left Peggy snoring in the backseat with her mouth open and her long hair all over the place, sweating on the vinyl upholstery. When we did see her later, she was with a group of her old friends from high school, all of them except Peggy holding babies or towing toddlers or both.

The two Kentucky state troopers who had been first on the scene the day before were there again. I overheard one tell Mr. Davis, the grocer, that more troopers would have come, but they were busy on the highways giving speeding tickets to holiday drivers and "mopping up" all the bad wrecks. "Probably going to be a lot more dead people on Kentucky roads today," he said, "than in this river."

At first light, the rubber-suited divers and the crane started working. In the red dawn the divers were like strangely dark and large river creatures in their wet suits, air tanks, fins, and masks, returning to the water after a nocturnal foraging of the land. The crane roared to life and swiveled its great arm out over the river, and the divers attached the large dangling hooks to something under the water.

The engine of the crane alternately sputtered and roared as a man in the cab of it pushed and pulled levers. The divers swam clear as the water came to life. Then the FRG bus broke the surface, a white whale. The crane lifted it higher and higher. It swayed as it dangled over the river, shedding water, and then moved toward the shore, a slow-moving flying albino dragon now instead of a whale, and people watched it, their mouths open, shading their eyes with a hand against the rising sun.

The crane set the bus down on its tires (which were not flat—a fact that for some reason surprised me) on the cracking, sunbaked river bank, looking pretty much as it had when it passed me on the road the day before, except that its bullet-shaped head lamps were askew and it looked cleaner, bathed—wet shiny in the sun.

The two state troopers shoved the folding door open and stepped up inside followed by two men, each carrying a body bag, from the Portsmouth funeral home (the Manchester funeral home didn't have the staff to handle all the sudden deaths in Devil's Elbow).

All movement and talk on the river bank stopped. Everyone froze in place to wait, silent, watching. The four men on the bus, visible through the windows, moved down the aisle to the back, looking left and right. They bent down, disappearing, then reappeared one by one.

An orange-headed kid about ten years old whispered to his buddy, "I wish they wouldn't put 'em in them bags first."

His buddy, who had a triangle of ringworms on his chin, nodded. "Yeah! I wanta see 'em."

Mama kept looking back and forth between me and the bus. I frowned at her. She didn't need to worry about me, I wanted to say, but I wasn't sure I could control my voice. If I spoke, it might come out loud and everybody would hear. The thick river air burned in my throat, and sweat rolled off me. My body started going numb, and spots all colors of the rainbow came into my eyes, and I sat down hard.

"Cadillac!" Mama said. "Honey!" I felt her hand on my shoulder and then against my cheek.

I sat, my head drooped, looking at the dry mud between my legs.

"There they is. Comin' out—" the orange-headed kid said. "Oh, man, I don't believe it!"

I looked up. The Portsmouth funeral-home men were walking back from the Frog bus with their body bags empty.

"Nothin!" the ringworm kid said. "I ain't got *all* day."

Orange said, "I'm hungry."

"I'm fine," I finally said to Mama as I thought about how the divers would have to go back down and look for the bodies of Kathy and her brother. I wondered whether they'd drifted down river and were tangled up in trash now, whether fish were nibbling on them or a boat had plowed into them, maybe chopped them up in its propellers.

Soon, a couple of kindergarten-age kids ventured

over and were sitting on the hood and roof of the bus, and soon enough other kids were inside it, sticking their heads out the windows, grinning and waving. The state troopers didn't seem to care.

A TV news crew—a camera guy and a reporter—from Cincinnati showed up early to shoot some footage. They were in a big hurry because they had to go film Fourth of July parades, car wrecks, and fireworks displays. A trooper brought them to me. They had me face the sun, which was still low in the sky, so it was like talking into a blinding spotlight. For some reason, I remembered something from Sunday school when I was little about a burning bush as I told about what I had seen on Devil's Elbow Road the day before and about running to the store to tell Mr. Lloyd. My chest hurt all over again, like I'd run hard in the heat again. My voice got shaky.

I didn't see the interview on the TV news that night, but Peggy let me know I looked like a dork and sounded like a girl.

My time in the spotlight would have been longer since I was the only eyewitness to the bus accident, but when they started pulling the other vehicles out of the river, my story was eclipsed.

The crane lowered its big hooks down to the divers

who disappeared under the water with them. In a few minutes, the divers re-appeared, gave a thumbs-up, and the crane chugged and sputtered and then roared with effort.

The river roiled. The divers swam toward the patrol boat a good distance away. The muddy river broke open and spewed up what looked like blood. Then something emerged. It looked like a raw bloody carcass. Then it transformed into the shiny red roof of a 1969 Buick Skylark. Then its white body was out of the water. It tilted, and water poured through the open driver's door, and the red and white vinyl upholstery was smooth and shiny, and the red steering wheel turned as the front white-wall tires cocked toward the crowd on the shore. The front end spun toward the crowd, and the sun caught the headlights, and it was like the driver was flashing his high beams (*Hey, how you doing?* Or: *Hey, look out. There's a cop around the bend*). People murmured. The chrome glistened. It was nicer than most cars folks around Devil's Elbow owned.

"Matt Braun," a man said.

"Who?" another man said.

"Shift manager at the lumber mill in Pig Gut."

"That his car?"

"I think so."

A third man said, "I'd know it anywhere."

"Fell off the face of the earth back in March."

"Fell off that cliff up there. That what he done."

The Skylark sailed toward us out of the sky, spun so that the rear was visible. The trunk was smashed in. Maybe the church bus had done that. The crane lowered the car slowly, maybe a hundred feet from the bus. When the Skylark landed, the tires flattened beneath its weight, and the trunk popped open. Everybody gathered around the trunk. Mama and I joined the crowd. I don't know what we expected to see, but it was just a trunk. Wet. A spare tire. A jack handle. We peered into the backseat. Nothing.

Maybe because Matt Braun was from Pig Gut, none of his family was present. A trooper wrote down the license-plate number. A little kid about six climbed into the passenger seat, grasped the steering wheel, and pretended to be driving and made high-pitched sounds suggesting speed and squealing tires. *Vroom! Screeeech!*

I didn't touch the car. I didn't understand the people touching it. A teenage boy reached into the trunk and took the jack handle when the troopers weren't looking and walked away with it down by the side of his leg. People sat on the hood.

Whenever there was a bad wreck around Elbow and a car got towed to Lloyd's garage while waiting to be hauled to the big junk yard in Manchester, people would go gawk at the twisted metal and shattered glass. Everybody thought the most interesting wrecked cars were the ones with blood smeared on the dashboard or a dark stain on a seat or dark red finger prints on a door handle. I didn't, but other kids entertained themselves with close scrutiny of wrecked cars and trucks. At school, they tried to describe the wrecks to me, but I didn't want to see them. I didn't like seeing the bus and the Skylark on the river bank. They represented death, and I had seen too much of death in the past twenty-four hours. Maybe somebody else's morbid curiosity would have been quenched by what I'd seen, but I'd never had much morbid curiosity.

The day promised bodies. The Skylark was just a preamble, a teaser. People were waiting to see Kathy and Kent Mayhew pulled up. And the first two divers who went down the day before and never returned. And they wanted to see more. Maybe skeletons. Real-life skeletons. Not plastic ones. The orange-headed kid and his buddy with the ringworms had disappeared for a while but were back.

The ringworm kid asked, "You think they'll still have clothes on? Or will they be naked?"

Orange said, "I think the catfish eat the clothes. The catfish eat everything. Clothes, shoes, belt buckles—"

"Belt buckles?"

"Yeah. Belt buckles. Watches. Then they eat the meat. You ain't gonna get to see no naked people. They gonna be nothin' but bones."

"If the catfish done ate the belt buckles, what makes you think they don't eat bones, too?"

"I guess they would. Yeah, they eat bones too."

"Man, you're bringin' me down. I'm gonna stop talkin' to you."

*** 

As much as everyone expected bodies, the morning progressed without a single one. A 1959 Plymouth was pulled up, the roof caved in, the windows all smashed. Then a 1952 Ford, the front fender dangling by one bolt. The reverse chronology of automotive history was broken by a 1956 Dodge.

A '69 Chevy Chevelle was parked up on Devil's Elbow Road at the cliff, a big chrome bumper peeking out over the edge. The Chevy's radio was turned up full blast, and the sound of The Doors floated down to us and across the water. "Mojo risin', mojo risin' ..."

There were no bodies, no skeletons, but there was usually somebody on the river bank when a car came out who recognized it: "That's Pat Walmack's Plymouth. He used to give me rides down to the sawmill when I worked there back in fifty-nine. He worked there too. Poor son a bitch."

But some of the cars were a mystery. An old man might mutter, "A '48 De Soto. Never seen that one before."

Miss Trout had made it to the riverbank, a little later than most. I figured she had to have walked all the way, and she moved pretty slow. She leaned on her thick gnarly walking stick and said, "Pat Walmack was gonna get hisself married in November '63, that Saturday after President Kennedy got hisself murdered. Mr. Walmack had to postpone his weddin'. Then he vanish and his girl done married a tractor salesman fella from Portsmouth."

A bearded old man wept at the sight of an old pick-up truck with spoke wheels twisting against the hot white sky like a hanged man. He turned and hollered to a group of women on the weedy ground above the bank, "He ain't comin' back now!" His eyes were shiny blue in a face the color of red brick. He turned back to the river and took a couple of steps into it, his blue trousers suddenly darkening, and his voice carried out over the water, "We love ya, Buck!"

More cars were dredged up. I didn't hear all the stories, but I saw people crying and hugging. After a car was set on the bank, they'd look it over, eyes wide, touch it, weep, then talk to a trooper, who wrote down what they told him.

Nan Mortimer, the reporter from Portsmouth who had written the story about Devil's Elbow that spring, was there and stuck around after all the other reporters left.

She stumbled up and down the river bank in her tight skirt and heels, looking as ever like Lois Lane, and she tried to interview nervous, crying people, and they tended to walk away without acknowledging her existence.

She held a tape recorder and I heard her say into it, "I'm here on the banks of the Ohio River in a place that some would say is appropriately named Devil's Elbow, and where today, on Independence Day, old mysteries are being dredged free from the muddy waters of the mighty Ohio. Mysteries solved. Secrets revealed."

Mama had not spoken much except to ask me twice whether I was okay. She watched the activity intently. As a rust-covered '50 Dodge swung in the air toward shore, she said, "It was a 1949 Mercury. Black."

"What was?" I asked.

"Your daddy's car."

"Oh." I had imagined a Cadillac for so long I was startled to hear her say his car was a Mercury.

Her face was already sunburned. Her eyes were alert, watching. She had put the scene at the Mayhews' behind her and had her vitality back.

"We made the payments late every month but . . . he loved it."

She took a deep breath. Sweat glistened on her brow. She looked at me but didn't say anything more. My God, I had never noticed how green her eyes were. She looked younger.

\*\*\*

The first of The Dead appeared not out of mist or under a full moon or in a wind storm. It was the Fourth of July at high noon with the sun blazing down. The crane hung over the river, the operator in the cab moving levers back and forth. The two divers were in the water. The two state troopers wearing sunglasses were watching the work. One of them noticed something and shouted, "Hey you! Lady! Get out of the river!"

Mama and I looked. After a glance, Mama looked back at the crane, which was pulling up another long-submerged vehicle. Maybe this one would be my father's, and Mama would know he hadn't abandoned her.

The person I saw—and it's important to emphasize it was what *I* saw because not everybody saw the same thing—emerging from the river was a tall, thin woman with black hair all the way down to her waist. Her narrow shoulders slumped as if with the weight of the river. Her dress was plastered to her shape. Her mouth hung wide open, extraordinarily wide. As she got closer, I saw that her jaw was unhinged. She couldn't close it. Her chin rested on her chest. Literally. Good God, it was awful, and other people who saw the same thing I did shrank back. All along one side of the woman's face was a deep gash. It didn't seem to be bleeding, but the center of it was juicy red. The edges were crusty black and the whole side of her face was purple. The inside of her mouth was wet pink and full of small gray teeth. At first, from where I stood on the bank, I thought she had no eyes, so small and colorless they were. But she started blinking and I saw that she did have eyes.

While others shrank back, Mr. Davis, the grocer, staggered down the bank toward her, gawking, his own mouth open but nothing like the woman's, his arms reaching out, his hands trembling. Her progress was slow but finally she had completely emerged and was standing on the shore with river water sloshing around her bare pink toes with long overgrown toenails, and Mr. Davis suddenly shouted, "Ma! Ma!"

I knew Mr. Davis well. Everybody did. He frowned at kids when they came into his store and watched us closely because he always thought we were going to steal Mountain Dews out of the barrel of ice he stocked daily or licorice sticks or moon pies. He was bald and looked older than the woman he was calling "Ma."

Mr. Davis lunged at her and embraced the dripping woman whose chin hung to her chest. He kissed the deep gash along her face, a long puckered kiss. He stroked her long sopping hair.

The trooper who had shouted at her came over to them, looked them over, his mouth open too. "My God, I'll call the life squad."

Mr. Davis just continued to embrace the woman. He muttered, "Ma," again.

The trooper said, "How did she get in the water? She your wife?"

I knew it wasn't his wife. Everybody knew his wife had died trying to have a baby twenty years ago.

Mr. Davis muttered, "Ma, Ma, Ma."

The trooper headed off to his patrol car to call for the county ambulance.

Mr. Davis shook his head, cried, and smiled. He caressed her mangled face. He cupped her chin in his hand, lifted it a little, then it fell back against her chest. She moaned, but it sounded more like a moan of pleasure than of pain. Her eyes closed, and I couldn't tell whether it was river water dripping from her face or tears.

"I've missed you so much, Ma. Where you been? How did you get here? Goodness gracious, you got wet, didn't you? Well, I don't blame you, it's hotter than hell out here. . . . Oh, I'm sorry, Ma. I know you don't like it when I use bad words. I won't again."

The other trooper was beside them now. "Did you fall, ma'am? You should sit down. Help will be here shortly, ma'am."

Then she looked at the trooper with those colorless

eyes of hers, and he stepped back. "Ma'am?"

Mr. Davis said through his tears, "My ma is fine. I'm going to take her home."

Miss Trout had made her way to them. She touched Mr. Davis' shoulder while she studied the woman he called "Ma." Miss Trout looked at the trooper, "I do think she fine. She not bleedin'. Her eyes bright as a cat's."

"What? You saying she always looks this way? These are *old* injuries?"

Miss Trout nodded. "Yes, um, I say they old."

"Maybe we should still take her to get checked out."

Mr. Davis sobbed, his chest heaving, and embraced his mother harder.

"Her son sure is upset. We better—"

"He just happy," Miss Trout said.

Mr. Davis squeezed his ma so hard river water squished out of her tattered dress that bore a faint floral pattern. The woman lifted her head back as though looking into the sun. Then she talked, to my surprise. Her tongue flicked around and she could even be understood: "My . . . son . . . will take . . . care . . . of me."

"Everything's gonna be good, Ma. Just like the old

days! Just like when I was little when it was just you and me, and Daddy wasn't around. And you don't ever have to worry 'bout Daddy again. Daddy's been dead ages."

"Take . . . me . . . home . . . Walter."

And they trudged up the bank, the trooper looking on, his hands on his hips, shaking his head. Others backed away and looked away. Old Man Whitaker, who had died the year before, had no lower jaw because he got cancer from chewing tobacco. Nobody could stand to look at him either. I figured something like the cancer had happened to the woman Mr. Davis thought was his ma.

I turned to Mama and said, "How she get in the water?"

"No idea." Like most of the people on the bank, Mama was now focused on the crane lifting another car out of the water. Only the rounded back of the vehicle had broken the surface. The bumper gleamed in the sunlight despite seeming to be nothing but rust.

"Why was Mr. Davis calling her Ma?"

Mama shrugged. "Sun can make people crazy. He probably got sunstroke. I see it at the hospital. Or he's drunk."

"Did he ever have a ma?"

"I always heard his mama ran off. Bout forty years ago. People say she drove off one night after her husband gave her a bad beatin'. Bill Davis was real mean, people say. And he drank, and that made it worse. Your daddy wasn't like that, though. Your daddy was a good man. He was a *real* man . . . muscles and a . . . and a rough beard . . ." —Mama was staring at the glittering river—"but not mean. Never mean."

I looked at her. She had just told me more about my father than she had my whole life.

The rest of the humpbacked car came out of the water and dangled against the blue sky. It was maybe from the late thirties. It clearly wasn't a 1949 Mercury.

"It will be the next one," Mama said. "I have a feeling."

The humpbacked car swung through the air and landed on the river bank next to the other vehicles, another pre-historic bird come to roost.

The divers got in the patrol boat and it sped off toward Manchester. The crane operator shut off the engine and climbed down from the cab and disappeared somewhere on the barge. It was lunch time. The state troopers left too. The life squad never came. I guessed the troopers radioed in to never mind. The reporters were long gone, except for Nan

Mortimer.

It was now very quiet without the roar of the crane and high buzz of the patrol boat. A breeze stirred, and it actually had a coolness to it, which made no sense.

The only people on the river bank now were the families of Devil's Elbow. The Dickers (mother, father, a boy in third grade and a boy in fifth grade) had built a camp fire and were roasting hot dogs and had a plastic ice chest full of RC Colas, Dr. Peppers, and Mountain Dews. In his deep Methodist Church choir voice, Mr. Dicker shouted up and down the river bank that they were selling a hot dog and a pop for a quarter to anyone who didn't want to go home for lunch. "Pop and a wiener!"

And while his voice echoed across the water— "wiener!!!!"—The Dead began to come out of the river one after another.

Mr. Lloyd's son, Jimbo.

The Kilpatricks' son.

The Jeffersons' grandpa.

Mrs. Stephens' daughter and son-in-law.

Mr. Adams' twin brother, who was an albino, but when he came out of the river he was the color of margarine.

A whole family that had vanished in 1951. The

Joneses.

An uncle of Miss Trout's who had gone missing in 1929.

Mrs. Dicker's daddy came up to her dripping and she dropped a wiener on his tattered, half-rotted shoe.

Other dead came that no one knew, people who had vanished in the river long ago and had no kin left in Devil's Elbow or weren't recognized by their descendants. Miss Trout had to tell who they were and direct them to the proper families. If there was no family, she adopted them on the spot. "You stick by me," she told them and patted their wet shoulders or arms.

There were a couple of strangers—Miss Trout swore they had never been citizens of Elbow. "Passin' through or lost. At night likely. No idea 'bout no hairpin turn."

The Dead staggered with broken limbs. Some had crushed skulls. Some had an eye missing. One had broken ribs poking out of his side. Their fingertips were black. They were gruesome monsters—except to those who remembered and loved them.

"My God, can't you see that he ain't got no nose?" Mrs. Lily O'Connor said to old Mrs. Stockard, who was passionately kissing the split lips of a young man wearing suspenders. She just kept kissing him. I could see her tongue in his mouth through the hole in his cheek.

Then Mrs. O'Connor glimpsed a man with half his gray brains exposed through a shattered skull, bits of bone dangling by threads of tissue and strands of hair, and she ran over and hugged him and shouted, "Daddy! Daddy!"

Mama gasped at the appearance of each of The Dead. They all looked horrible to her. They all looked horrible to me.

Mr. Black, the minister from the Frog church, shouted, "It's the end of the world! Prepare to be taken up to Heaven!" Then he saw his lost sixteen-year-old daughter coming out of the river—missing for a decade—and he ran to her, "An angel!" And embraced her shattered body. She wore shorts and a halter top, and bones poked through the split skin of her arms and legs. An ear dangled by a thread of raw pink skin. "An angel!" Then he muttered, "Oh, baby girl, you got to get some decent clothes on."

And for the first time in my life, I heard Mama swear. "What the hell?"

Members of the Frog church were on their knees

praying or writhing in the dirt and speaking gibberish, terrified of the work of the Devil—until their own loved ones emerged from the water. Then it was all "Praise, Jesus!"

Then the Frogs became split on whether this was the work of God or Satan. One man started waving his pocket-size Bible and quoting chapter and verse—"So saith the Lord . . . ." Another man squared off against him with a larger, burgundy-bound edition and his own passages of choice. Both men had crew-cuts and stocky builds. They might have been brothers. They started circling each other, both of them stumbling on riverbank trash—bottles, cans, drift wood. Then one threw a punch and they ended up jabbing at each other, both crouched low like Sonny Liston or Rocky Marciano. The men's wives, in long Frog dresses, started pulling each other's long hair from their buns and then rolled around in the dried mud, their dresses hiked up to reveal their thick thighs and white cotton panties. All four of them got worn out after about one minute—it wasn't like in the movies at all, where fights went on for about fifteen minutes—and the quartet collapsed onto the ground and cursed at each other like sixth graders ("You suck donkey dicks") while they tried to catch their breath.

\*\*\*

Unexpected clouds had come into the sky. Nothing dark or threatening. Wispy clouds but enough to block the sun and give some relief and clearer vision without all the glare. A breeze stirred again. And another figure rose from the river. It was Kathy Mayhew.

I stared. I glanced away at the bus sitting cockeyed on the river bank. I looked back. She was coming.

And she looked perfectly fine, just wet, the way people did when preachers dunked them in the river for baptism.

A girl from our school shouted, "Kathy!" and started to run out to her, but the girl's mother pulled her back. No one approached her. She was being shunned, maybe because of what her mother had done. So I walked toward her. Our eyes locked and we got closer and closer. When we were only inches apart we stopped. "Hi," I said.

"You're Cadillac."

I nodded. "Hey, Kathy."

"You go to my school."

"I sit behind you in—"

"I know. I always hear you breathing back there."

And her saying that made me wonder whether she

was breathing, and I watched her chest, and she was. She looked fine in every way. Her sopping pale-green dress molded around her small breasts. She looked beautiful.

"You want to come get a hot dog and a pop? I got money. The Dickers are—"

"What happened?"

"What? What do you mean?"

"Why was I in the river? How did I get there?"

"You don't remember?"

"Why are all these people here?"

"Because . . . . It's . . . it's the Fourth of July."

I was trying to figure out how to tell her everything, but then her brother came up out of the river. "Kent!" she cried. "Are you all right?"

"Yeah, I'm okay," he said. "Why?"

But he didn't look okay. He looked as though every bone in his face was broken. His nose was smashed to one side; his eyes weren't aligned with each other; his cheeks were purple with bruises and cuts; his chin was split open. When he talked, his lower lip separated grotesquely, half of it moving, half not moving.

He staggered up to us, and Kathy ruffled the wet hair atop that mutilated face and said, "Good. Except you're all wet, you dork."

"You are too, *dork*." He stuck out his tongue and half of it was missing.

I stepped back. Kathy looked at me. "You look like you're gonna puke."

I swallowed hard. "Your brother really looks all right to you? You don't see . . . ?"

"What are you talking about?"

"I'm talking about his . . . face."

"He's always been an ugly little creep."

I gawked at her. "How do all these people around us look?" I pointed at Jimbo, Mr. Lloyd's son. "Like him." I pointed at Mr. Black's daughter. "And her."

"They're all wet looking."

"What else?"

"They're just wet looking. Everybody getting baptized?"

"They don't look hurt? Injured?"

"No. How do I look?"

I looked her up and down. "You look real nice."

She smiled. "Then why you askin'? And why are me and Kent here. We're not Baptists."

Bobby Rose, a kid Kent's age, ran up to him. "Hey, Kent, you wanta a wiener?" And the kid held out a bunless hot dog like it was his pecker. "Eat me." Then he ran away and Kent ran after him.

"See," Kathy said. "Kent's fine."

I looked around.

The Elbowers who had stayed there on the river bank, the ones who had not fled in horror, seemed to be adjusting to the mix of gruesome Dead and okay-looking Dead surrounding them. Everybody seemed to see only some of the Dead as gruesome and some as perfectly fine looking. When you live in a town where an old woman has boils all over her face and a man has no jaw because of cancer and several men are missing limbs or half their face because of the wars or farm machinery or the saw mill and all kinds of people have no teeth, The Dead don't seem so strange.

When I was in elementary school, a kid had a hump on his narrow back near his left shoulder blade that was his parasitic twin. On the playground behind a huge and gnarly cottonwood he'd take his shirt half off, and you could see that the hump had little arm-like nubs—they were rat arms—and a small nub in the center was his twin's nose. That's what the boy said. He was gone after third grade because he and his parents joined a travelling carnival.

There were plenty of Living who looked nearly as

bad as The Dead. But were The Dead really dead? No. Hell no. They were walking and talking, so no. Kathy was definitely not dead. She was fine and looked fine.

I put off explaining anything to her and bought her a hot dog and a Dr Pepper.

All up and down the river bank beneath Devil's Elbow Road, The Living and The Dead were eating hot dogs together and guzzling sodas.

The number of Dead rising from the river had tapered off. Only occasionally now did a Dead emerge.

"Cadillac!" Mama called. I was staring at Kathy at the moment. She had a blood-like drop of ketchup at the corner of her mouth, and I was fantasizing about how I would remove it for her. I could reach out with a napkin and dab at it. Or I could use the tip of my finger and gently wipe it away and then lick it off my finger. Or I could lean toward her slowly, saying something silly like, "Don't move. I've seen a doctor do this on TV," and I'd part my lips just a little as they met hers . . . .

"Cadillac!"

But Mama interrupted all that. Her voice was at my ear now, and then I felt her hand on my shoulder or at least I thought it was *her* hand. I turned and looked into a stranger's face—half of which was stripped of flesh to the shiny white bone. The remaining flesh was ragged and bruised and blistered. Tiny black bugs swarmed over a hole where the nose should have been. The eyes were yellow and cockeyed. The wasted lips turned up in a wild and horrible grin of jagged brown teeth and bloody gums.

"My boy!"

I fell back away from the skeletal hand on my shoulder and gawked up from the ground at this figure.

Mama turned to him, touched his upper arm, and said, "It's just such a shock, babe. He doesn't remember you at all, you know."

This figure my mama had just called "babe" nodded. "I understand. This is a shock for me too."

"Cadillac was just tiny."

"He's a big boy now." Blood-filled eye sockets looked me up and down. Of all The Dead, my father was the most gruesome.

My father.

This really was my father before me. When I had been little, I had fantasized about tossing a football with him, about going fishing together, about watching Cincinnati Reds baseball games on TV, maybe even going to a game one day at old Crosley Field.

Mama took his arm and said, "We should get you home and into some dry clothes. I have some of your clothes in a bag in the back of our closet."

He was still studying me. "Okay, son. We'll see you later at home. I know I must look a fright all wet like this." His jaw clicked when he spoke.

Then his bloody sockets slid to Kathy. "Girlfriend?"

Kathy blushed instantly, looked down shyly at his rotted shoes.

Mama frowned and looked Kathy up and down as though she didn't like what she saw.

Dead Dad grinned gruesomely, maybe even lecherously at Kathy, but it was hard to tell since he was missing half his face.

Mama tugged on his arm and they turned away. I watched them.

Then I looked at Kathy, who still had the ketchup at the corner of her mouth and who said, "Your mom and dad seem nice."

"Yeah. My mama's okay. I don't really know my dad."

"I know what you mean. Ever since I turned

twelve, my parents have been so different. I just want to say to them, 'Who are you people?'"

"I've never known my dad at all. He's always been gone."

"My dad worked in a coal mine in West Virginia for a year. He only came home like one day a month. Made good money but my mom made him quit 'cause she couldn't stand him being away. She got awful sad and she'd just sit around in her nightgown all day and wouldn't take a bath and completely ignored me and Kent."

"My mom's been sad about my dad all my life."

"He cheat on her? I can see how he would have the opportunity."

"The opportunity?"

"I mean, he's just such a good looking man."

"He is?"

"You look a lot like him."

"Oh."

She drank the last of her pop, her head back, and I watched her neck and imagined leaning toward her and kissing her smooth, white pulsating throat.

She looked at me. "One time I heard my mom tell my dad if he ever cheated on her she'd kill him with his own shotgun."

I stared at her. I didn't know what to say.

"Anyway, me and Kent should go home. Mom will be having a fit if she doesn't know where we are. She'll call the sheriff. No kidding. I mean it. She will. She has. I mean, she really did one time."

"No! You don't wanta go home. She knows where you are. She was here."

"It's so weird not to remember how I got here."

"It's probably just . . . just those things in health class."

"What?"

"You know, like what we learned in health class. Kids our age . . . . Especially girls . . . ."

"Hormones?" she said.

"Yeah, hormones. Mrs. Phillips says they make you crazy." I quickly added, "Not . . . not that I think . . . . I mean, I don't think you're crazy." I said it really seriously.

She grinned and rolled her eyes. "You're funny."

Kent ran up with one of his friends, and all out of breath, he said, "Hey, dork, I'm gonna over to Timmy's." His shattered face glistened with sweat.

"Does Mom know?"

"She won't care." And he and Timmy took off.

"Yes, she will!" Kathy shouted after him. "You

know she will!"

Kent ignored her.

I looked around. Most people had left. Living and Dead. The troopers and the divers were just getting back from lunch. "Come home with me," I said.

"I don't know," she said, looking around.

"Come on. I'll be funny some more."

"My house is on the way. We can stop and ask Mom and Dad."

"Okay. But they . . . they might not be home."

***

I didn't know what would happen when we got to her house. I hoped it would look empty and she'd be willing to just walk by.

I said something dumb like, "You like school?" And then even dumber, "What do you want to be when you grow up? I mean, when you finish school?"

She answered quickly. "All I know is I wanta move away from here. I wanta get a billion miles away from my mom and dad. They gotta know where I am every second. They think I'm going to take up smoking and drinking moonshine and putting on nail polish as soon as I can get out of their sight. It's because of that church they make me go to. I know everybody calls us Frogs. I wanta get two billion miles away from that

111

church. You go to church?"

"Naw." I kicked at loose chunks of the gray crumbling, tarry pavement as we began our climb up Devil's Elbow Road. Some melted asphalt stuck to my tennis shoe.

"Soon as I'm eighteen, I'm hittin' the highway. It'll be *my* highway. Maybe the highway to Hell but at least it'll be mine. That church is all about *their* way or the *Hell* way. That's what they say. 'Our way or the Hell way.' Have you ever heard anything so stupid?"

"My mama pretty much gave up on church after my dad left."

"I wish *my* dad would leave. Mom too."

Then there it was. Her house.

There was yellow crime-scene tape around the front porch, like you see on TV shows.

"What the—?" she said. I reached for her but she was already gone, and I just stood in the road and watched. She ran up on the porch and tore the tape apart and burst inside. I watched that tape flutter to the ground and lie there limply. It lay there for a minute. Then a breeze caught it, lifted it up, and it flew away from the house until it snapped taut. It was tethered to a porch post and writhed and snapped again and again in the sudden breeze.

I stayed in the hot road. The open front door of the Mayhew home was a black hole. Not a sound came from the house. There was no telling what was in there. I doubted anyone had cleaned anything up.

Then Kathy stepped back out onto the porch and stood there, her eyes staring at nothing at first. Then she looked at the yellow writhing crime-scene tape. She stared at the tape big-eyed, then squinted at it, then started nodding her head.

I stood, my hands opening and closing at my sides. My heart pounded.

When she stopped nodding, she let loose with the worst sounds I'd ever heard. I had witnessed the slaughter of hogs and rabbits and cows, and I'd seen dogs and cats get hit by cars or shot by mean drunks. I heard a man beating his wife and kids and seen lots of horror movies. But I had never heard the kinds of sounds Kathy made. A dying rabbit was the closest thing—the worst kind of baby's screams you can imagine.

# DAY THREE
## *The Preacher's Resurrection*

The next morning I woke up on the floor in the front parlor of my house. We called it the TV room. It had seventy-year-old faded wallpaper (big pink roses on thorny green stems) peeling off the walls and a tarnished brass chandelier with only one light bulb working. The plaster ceiling was crisscrossed with cracks that looked like a Kentucky roadmap—lots of twists and turns and dead ends.

I felt like I'd been trampled by a stampede of wild boars, the kind that lived in the woods around Devil's Elbow. They were the descendants of escaped domestic pigs that quickly transformed from smooth and pink creatures like in the illustrations of *Charlotte's Web* into huge and hairy monsters with tusks. Rolly Dinkman shot one in '64 that weighed out at over twelve hundred pounds. Turd Tuttle claimed he saw one that must have weighed at least two thousand and that its hide was so tough the bullets from Turd's .22 just bounced off.

Lying there on the parlor floor that morning, I felt transformed. In no way was I a boy anymore. And like those escaped pigs, I felt like I was transforming into something rough and bristly. I had all my sweat-stiff clothes on, except for my shoes, which served as my smelly pillows.

I lay flat on my back and had trouble remembering the night before.

I was alone in the parlor, and the French doors were closed. One of our cats hopped through the empty space where the pane of glass was missing, dropped a dead field mouse beside my face, and meowed at me. Mom would have yelled at the cat for bringing the nasty thing in the house. Peggy would have screamed bloody murder. I rubbed the cat's head and thanked her. The cats just wanted attention sometimes. The dead mouse was a gift. It lay on its back, its eyes closed, its head lolling. The cat could have eaten it, but chose to give it to me. I rubbed her head again, and she purred. Damn, I was sentimental that morning, especially for somebody who felt as gross as I did. Then the cat touched the mouse's head, and the thing turned out not to be dead after all. It opened its eyes, flipped itself onto its feet, and shot away across the room and under the French doors.

The cat took off after it.

I got up off the floor and sniffed my underarms. I smelled like death. I walked down the hall to the old music room, which was Mama's bedroom. We didn't use the upstairs—too hot in the summer and impossible to heat in the winter, not to mention all the leaks that came through the ceiling when the rain buckets in the attic overflowed. Mama's door was shut, but I pushed it open quietly. It was a big room with a nineteenth-century grand piano in the corner. The black finish of the piano was crackled. The legs always reminded me of the legs of a fat woman in a carnival. Mama was asleep on the bed, her hair all tangled up above her head like a mushroom cloud from an atomic bomb. She was alone. Maybe I had only dreamed about my father coming back.

Down the hall from Mama's room was the only bathroom. It didn't have a shower, just an old claw-foot cast-iron tub. The pipes rattled and groaned, and I had to let the water run a long time before it turned warm. Then I took off my clothes and washed myself quickly because I wanted to see whether Kathy was waking up.

I put on my jeans from the day before and went down the hall bare-chested. I was skinny and had a tan, but it bothered me that I was so hairless. Jake Holden, a kid at school, had tufts of black fur sprouting from the top of his shirt when he was fourteen, and he got a three-o'clock shadow every day. I was sixteen, and I didn't even need to shave more than once a fortnight. I still don't.

I looked in my room, which was originally a library with floor-to-ceiling book shelves stocked with moldy hundred-year-old books of all kinds—everything from law books and novels with gilded page edges to ledger books full of carefully printed numbers and names written in a neat and fancy cursive. Most of the books were bound in leather and were so old the leather was disintegrating. Whenever I pulled one off a shelf, my hands got dirty from a kind of powder the leather was crumbling into. Still, I liked the old books and sometimes I found century-old dried flower petals or four-leaf clovers pressed between the pages or a lock of hair from some long-dead relative or maybe from the lover of a long-dead relative. It was weird to me that these things existed so long after the person was gone. Maybe the lock of hair was taken from a corpse, and a grief-stricken relative or lover sat around caressing that lock of hair and remembering and missing the dead person, stunned and disbelieving that the person was really gone—gone forever, never to be seen again, never to speak again.

The afternoon before, Kathy would occasionally plea through her sobs, "I want my mom and dad back. Please! I want them back." And then demand, "I want them *back!*"

For a long time, we sat on the side porch of my house, away from the front where neighbors, strangers, and Dead folks were coming and going. After a while she was silent for maybe a half hour until she said, "Tell me everything. Don't leave anything out."

I did my best to tell her about it all—the bus going over the cliff, Mr. Lloyd, The Preacher, the state troopers, the divers, her mom coming to the river bank, even what I had seen at her house that morning.

She nodded a few times, her face ashen, her eyes wide but without tears.

When it started to get dark, we heard fireworks in the distance, but we didn't bother to look for the bursting tendrils in the sky. There were always displays upriver in Portsmouth and in Maysville that could be seen for miles.

When some of the people who were coming and

going from my house started setting off firecrackers in the yard and the noise and smell made Kathy twitch, I took her inside to my room and told her to make herself at home. I told her she could look at the old books if she wanted to.

But this morning she wasn't in there. I worried that she'd left and I was horrified to think she'd go to her house full of blood stains and brain matter.

I thought I heard a noise from upstairs and figured birds had gotten in again through the chimneys or broken windows, but I hoped it was Kathy looking around. I just didn't want her to be gone. Then I heard soft voices in the kitchen. I put on a clean shirt and headed to the back of the house.

I stood at the closed kitchen door, trying to identify the voices, but they were low mutters. I pushed on the door and peeked in, and they all stopped talking and stared at me. Kathy sat at one end of the table across from my father, and in the middle was a stranger, a young lanky guy who didn't look much older than Peggy. He wore a funny-looking half-rotted suit and bowtie. A chunk of bone from his forehead was missing so that his brain was visible.

My father turned his red-and-black eye sockets my way and said, "Mornin', son!"

I stepped into the room. "Ya'll been up long?"

"We can't . . . we couldn't sleep, son."

I nodded slowly. "You feeling better?"

They all nodded, although the question was intended for Kathy.

I hadn't seen Peggy the night before or Mama, but I remembered Mama's door being closed.

Now at the kitchen table, Kathy looked more like her normal self and she said, "Thank you for letting me have your room, Cadillac."

"Oh, you're welcome. You can sleep in my room any time."

Dad gestured, a wave of his skeletal hand. "Come here, son. Come sit down."

The table had nothing on it. No cups, no plates. "Ya'll want coffee or something?" I asked.

"No, son. Just come sit down."

I sat across from the stranger.

Dad said, "This is Paul. Dr. Paul Urbinsky. He's from up round Pittsburgh. Traveling through on his way to his first job at Mercy Hospital in Cincinnati. Got lost, though."

"Glad to meet you, Dr. Urbinsky," I said, my eyes on his pink and pulsating brain.

"Glad to meet you, Cadillac. You can call me Dr.

Paul. A lot easier to say. I just graduated from the medical school at UP. University of Pittsburgh." His eyes went crossed. "Not *just*, I suppose. A while back . . . now." His brain rippled.

Dad said, "Dr. Paul is confused. Matter of fact, I'm confused. Your little girlfriend here is too."

I nodded. "Yeah, I think everybody's kind of confused."

Dad turned his bloody eye sockets toward me squarely. "Kathy says it's 1971. The *year* 1971."

"Yeah, it is."

"Dr. Paul got lost in 1923. Last thing he remembers before yesterday is driving down Devil's Elbow Road at night, though he didn't know the name of it. The last thing that *I* remember is it was 1955. A blazin' hot Sunday. Hot as yesterday."

"Yeah," I said, nodding hard. "Then yesterday you came walking out of the river. You all did."

"But that don't make no sense. Where have I been? Where have all of us been? We don't remember anything. . . ."

"I think it had something to do with The Preacher." I looked at Kathy. "The one that visited your bible school."

Her eyes got big. "Yeah, that real old creepy man.

He talked about letting snakes and rats crawl all over him."

I looked at Dad and then at Dr. Paul, whose brain was twitching. "The Preacher stood in the river and prayed and then he talked in tongues. Then—" I looked around at them all with my mouth hanging open.

"Then what?" Dad asked.

"Then he died. He dropped over. He's . . . he's dead. He was talking in tongues standing there in the river and he fell over dead."

"Dead?"

I quickly added, "But maybe he'll come back to life. You were dead too. I think."

Dad frowned at me as best he could with half a face, and Dr. Paul's brain pulsated like water coming to a boil.

"That's impossible," Dr. Paul said. "Dead is dead. I've seen lots of corpses during my medical training. I dissected them, performed autopsies, and—"

"Yeah," Dad said. "We're not dead. People don't just come back from bein' dead, son. Not after years. Decades. I remember my grandmother droppin' over in this very kitchen and my parents thought she was gone for sure. Limp as a fish. No breath. No heartbeat.

Then she opened her eyes. But that was only about two minutes that she seemed gone and she wasn't really. She couldn't have been, though she did say she talked to God while she was passed out and He told her to go back." Daddy was shaking his head.

I sat there looking at two gruesome corpses. Walking, talking corpses, yes, but obviously corpses.

"I'm not either," Kathy said. "Dead."

"No, you're not. You're obviously not. But look at your brother."

"There's nothing wrong with Kent."

"There's nothing wrong with me either," Dad said.

"Or me. I'm a physician. I'd know if I were dead." His brain swelled out of that hole in his forehead.

"You don't see anything wrong with yourselves?"

"Like what?" Dad asked.

"You don't have a nose, Dad!" I turned to Dr. Paul. "You've got a hole in the front of your head the size of a baseball."

"Boy, what're you talkin' 'bout? Dr. Paul here looks as normal and healthy as I do."

I gawked at him. Then I looked at Kathy, who said, "Didn't we cover this subject yesterday at the river?"

"You really don't see it? Not your brother? Not my dad or Dr. Paul? Everybody looks fine to you?

123

Nobody at this table has a messed up face?"

Kathy frowned at me. "*You've* got a few zits."

I sputtered. "Dad. Where have you been since 1955? Dr. Paul? How about you? Since what? 1923? Where you been? And if it's 1971, Dr. Paul, why aren't you *old*?"

***

We were sitting there in silence when we heard a vehicle backfiring again and again. Each explosion was like a shotgun blast.

Then we heard singing. Loud. A bunch of people. The singing was off key and ragged, and the voices were not in sync. They weren't even all singing the same lyrics.

I got up and looked out the window. It was a beat-up black truck, a 1946 Ford belching black smoke. Its muffler hung loose, and when the truck hit a bump, the muffler scraped the asphalt and shot off a shower of sparks. It was a hog-hauling truck with wooden sides and a wooden gate. It was full of Dead men and women standing in the back, holding onto the railings and singing gospel. The truck staggered up into our yard and stopped with a banshee screech of its worn-out brakes. The rusty driver's door swung open with another screech, and out popped The

Preacher. He was naked as a jaybird.

\*\*\*

My first thought was not to step outside but to go hide and wait for them to go away. The Preacher showing up spooked me worse than anything else that had happened. Maybe it was because I had seen him die. His death was more of a reality for me than the deaths of the others. If there had been any lingering doubt about people coming back from death, this sealed the deal—people died but then they came back to life. It could happen. It *did* happen. Also, The Preacher's nudity was somehow worse than all the rotted flesh and exposed bones, sinews, and brains of The Dead.

I was still at the window, off to the side and behind the red-and-white checkered curtain so as not to be seen, when I saw my father, Dr. Paul, and Kathy out in the yard. I hadn't realized they'd left the kitchen.

I knew I had to go outside or I'd revert back into a little kid. I said out loud to myself, "Don't be a pussy, Cadillac."

I had put on a short-sleeve dress shirt, and for some reason, I felt the need to tuck in my shirt tails. When I stepped outside, The Preacher's attention was immediately drawn to me like I was the one person

125

he'd been searching for: "How are you, boy? Ain't it glorious!"

He came to me and put his arm around my shoulder and squeezed me like I was his son. He smelled funny, I thought. There was the smell of hospital disinfectant about him but also a hint of river water and fish. His skin was all wrinkly white and covered in moles and age spots, and his body hair was white. He had a long and thick silver scar that ran diagonally across his belly and another scar the size of a silver dollar on his right thigh.

He caught me staring at his scars.

"The Great War, so called," he explained. "World War One. Should have been called the Devil's War. I have had dreams 'bout Hell being like those killing fields in France."

"Jim Morrison died in France," I said for some pointless reason.

"Lot of men did. Yellow clouds of gas. Men coughing up their lungs. Blood running out of their every orifice. That's how it was in France in 1918. In my dreams of Hell the men don't die. They just cough and cough and bleed and vomit."

All The Dead who had come in the hog hauler with him gathered round. I found myself surrounded by them, and they pressed in closer and closer during his silent reflection on the war in France. His eyes had wandered down to the dirt and dead grass at his blue-veined feet.

Then he lifted his eyes slowly until they latched onto mine again like tractor beams on the TV show *Star Trek*. "You do hear me now, right?"

He waited.

A Dead person behind me softly said, "Answer him, boy."

I nodded.

"But do you *see it*?" The Preacher asked.

I nodded again.

"Can you *smell* it?"

I blinked. Then I shrugged.

"Can you smell the sulfur and brimstone of hot guns and exploding shells? A million whiffs of brimstone. And the cigarette smoke—all that cigarette smoke. Sweet French tobacco. The men all smoked constantly. The plumes rose from a trench so great you'd think it was a cloud of the mustard gas. They smoked so they'd not smell the other smells. Do you know what the other smells were, boy?"

I slowly shook my head.

"The stench of human waste . . . and putrefied

flesh." He was looking at the ground again, maybe at the black, cracked toenail on his left foot. Then he slid his eyes up to me again. "Bodies lay for days. You couldn't get to them. When you could and you'd bury them, the Germans shot mortars at you that shook the earth and rattled your brains. Made you shit yourself and loosened your teeth so that they started falling out of your head. And the mortars kept coming, and they made you deaf so that everybody round you became a mime and your head buzzed . . . and all those dead men you buried were blown up out of their graves. . . . They were all back. All those dead men had returned." He paused to look around at his truck load of Dead. "But they weren't pretty like these folks." He sighed long and hard.

"Praise Jesus," muttered a Dead woman with empty eye sockets.

"Machine-gun fire. That's what got me. I died in the mud of that hellish field in France." Then The Preacher flung his fist in the sky like he was trying to punch a hole through a cloud, and his old flesh rippled and flapped, and he started talking fast. "I *shot* like a Fourth of July rocket straight through a tunnel dark as a movie house with flashes of my life going through my head all the way. I saw my grandmother rocking on our porch. I saw my mother baking bread. My father taking a razor strop to me. . . . A young, young girl I loved. Oh, God, I *loved* her. She smelled like lilacs. I heard my favorite song—a church hymn. I patted my favorite dog."

His hand moved in the air like he was petting that dog again.

"I smelled my old baseball mitt. That wonderful leather smell. Then I was in a great hall of light at the foot of God, and the Lord said *unto me*: 'Go back! Go back, young man, and make use of your earthly time saving souls in My name.' Then The Lord reached toward me and touched my chest where my heart is, and I woke up in a trench surrounded by dead soldiers, and I had to hold my organs in with my hands, and my thigh bone glistened in the French sunshine that shined somehow through all the smoke. The Lord did that."

He nodded, bit his lip like he was about to cry. "The surgeon at the field hospital wouldn't let the stretcher bearers take me into the operating tent. That doctor told them to put me out with the dead. He told them there was nothing he could do for me. So they laid me outside out of the way surrounded by corpses, and all of a sudden, it started to rain, just a sprinkling at first, like how some of the churches sprinkle you for baptism, and every few minutes, those stretcher bearers walked past me to stack corpse upon corpse, and I was groaning and speaking in tongues. Then it started to rain harder, like the full emersion baptism that the righteous perform. And I kept talking in tongues. The rain drops that fell upon me glowed because the light of God was inside me, and I lay there all lit up. It was like I'd been poured full of radium. Then I started singing with the glowing rain running down my face, and the rain filled my blasted-out gut and my blasted-out thigh, and the music that came out of my throat was beautiful. I had never sung that way before and I have never sung that way since. I couldn't carry a tune before and haven't been able to carry a tune since, but I sang like an angel that day. And the stretcher bearers picked me up and took me into the tent, yelling, 'Doc, you got to shut him up! He won't stop singing!'

"The surgeon looked up from a slab of meat, his hands all covered in blood like he was a mad butcher, and I saw all this from a distance, from up in the sky, and he said, 'Get rid of this one and bring me Al Jolson over here and lay him down. Jesus Christ, he's full of rain water.'"

The Preacher paused, nodded. The Dead surrounding us were silent, except for their breathing. Some sounded normal, inhaling and exhaling quietly. Others were raspy, or things rattled inside them.

"As soon as I woke up out of the operating gas, I started saving souls. A nurse came to my bed and said, 'I see you're back with us, private.' And I said, 'Do you know the Lord, ma'am? Come kneel and pray with me, ma'am.'"

One, then two, then three of The Dead said, "Amen."

"I saved 'em left and right in that Army hospital—twenty-six or seven boys my age—cynical boys with body parts missing—and four or five nurses, even a doctor. On the ship back home to America, I saved more souls. I held prayer meetings on the deck. I saved people on the docks in New York City and a hundred more as I hitchhiked home on crutches from New York to West Virginia. I have saved thousands of souls over the years. And think if the lord had not sent me back. *Think* of it! A lot of those souls I saved have passed on—I'm an old man now. Thousands of souls might be burning in Hell—in that Hell of mustard gas and never-ending agony—instead of basking in Heavenly light."

He raised his eyes to the gloomy sky, the sun nowhere in sight. "The Lord spared me then and he has spared me again! Hallelujah!"

"Hallelujah!" shouted The Dead.

I blinked at him. When the hallelujahs died down, I said, "Why are you naked?"

He gave me a look of amazement. His mouth hung open so wide I could count all the gold fillings in his teeth.

The Dead woman with empty eye sockets said, "You must be blind, boy. This man is cloaked in The Robes of Glory."

I shook my head a little and muttered to The Preacher, "Everybody can see your privates."

I know it sounds like I was trying to be funny, but I wasn't.

"Don't be ridiculous." He spun around, his pecker swinging. He had a huge one, and I wondered if that was usual for preachers. I'd heard that women liked preachers and that preachers got loved up more than regular men. Women liked a man with a silver tongue, the gift of eloquent speech, people said. But maybe it was their big peckers too.

"No, you're naked as a jaybird," I said flatly.

Dr. Paul had come up and was standing next to me and said, "No, Cadillac. My God! He's wearing shining golden robes. It's like he's wearing the sun!"

All I saw was saggy old skin, moles, white body hair and that huge swinging dick.

A fat woman in a dark-green dress torn across her torso revealing a mostly severed breast spoke up: "He done raised us all from death! Hallelujah!" Then she dropped to her knees, her left breast held by barely a shred of skin. "Praise Him. For he is The Lord!"

"Yes, The Lord!" another Dead woman said and dropped to her knees.

A man whose forehead was cracked like a shattered car windshield dropped to his knees too: "This preacher is Jesus."

Another Dead man dropped to his literally skeletal knees, threw up boney arms, wiggled boney fingers, and shouted, "Praise Jesus!"

Then there was general clamor: "The Second Coming!"

"Jesus has returned!"

"'And he shall raise up the dead unto Heaven.'"

The Preacher turned and smiled at his disciples, his dick swaying.

A Living man in white hospital pants and a white shirt pushed his way to the front of the group and stood next to The Preacher. "I seen him"—and he jabbed a finger at The Preacher—"come back alive." He nodded emphatically. "I work in the morgue in Manchester, and I seen hundreds of dead folk the last nineteen years. Maybe thousands. And I never seen none come back alive. Until last night. I seen this preacher man brought in. I *helped* bring him in. I stripped him of his wet clothes and positioned his limbs on the gurney. He was *gray*. He had them dark gouges under his eyes that dead folk get and the blood had settled into his fingernails. I combed his hair back and left him in the corner. Later, I'm sweepin' the floor and I hear a moan that about made me soil myself, and there he is! Sittin' up on that Goddamned gurney. And he *looked* at me." He grinned, showing that he had some teeth missing and that the ones he did have were gruesome yellow. "And I pissed myself! Look!" He pointed to the yellow stain on the front of his white pants. "Sittin' up on his gurney, his sheet throwed off on the floor. And he's pink and as alive as me or that cat there." He pointed at the cat that had brought me a mouse as a present that morning. The cat rubbed against the man's shin. "And I fell to my knees before him. And he said, 'Get me a bus or a van or a truck.' And I did. I right away stole—ah, borrowed—this here truck."

The Preacher slapped the man on the back. "Let us sing, brothers and sisters. Let us raise our voices to Heaven so that we may follow our words up into the sky and be closer to The Father."

I wanted to ask the morgue worker from the hospital what he saw The Preacher wearing, but he was singing his head off with the rest of them, something about 'Take me, O Lord, up to the green pastures.'"

Peggy came outside and hollered to me above the singing: "I never heard such caterwaulin', and why's that old man naked?"

I turned to her and wanted to hug her but didn't. "Thank God, you're seeing the same thing I am. Everybody else says he's got gold robes on."

She scrunched up her face. "He's gross. I never seen anybody with so many moles."

"Yeah, he's naked all right. That's what I was trying to tell Dr. Paul—"

"Oh, Paul! Yeah. I think he kind of likes me. We talked a long time last night. He's kind of goofy but in a cute way. Kind of like Ringo Starr."

"Peggy—"

"I'm gonna tell him I need a check-up."

"His brains are hanging out."

"Yeah, he's gotta be real smart. He's a doctor. But he's real young. And good looking."

"He looks like . . . like a corpse!"

"No, you must be talkin' about your girlfriend."

"What?"

"That girl you brought home. Talk about rode hard and put up wet. I hope you know what a rubber is for."

"What are you talking about?"

"Jesus, Cadillac. She looks—"

"Hi, Peggy." It was Dr. Paul with a big grin on his gray face. His brain seemed to be sweating.

"Oh, hi, Paul. Sorry I fell asleep last night. I just couldn't stay awake. Probably all that sun I got yesterday." She winced. "Or maybe I have something really wrong with me. I been havin' these aches down here in my belly. Way down." She touched herself with her fingertips just south of her belly button.

I walked away. I found Kathy around on the side porch. She looked beautiful. She was just sitting there in a wicker rocking chair, not rocking, staring off into space.

"You okay?"

She shook her head. "No."

"What's wrong?" I sat down at her feet, looking up at her.

"Well . . . for starters . . . my mom killed my dad and then herself. And me and Kent don't have any grandmas or aunts or anybody. And I'm not letting any of those Frogs adopt us. We're gonna end up in that big old orphanage everybody talks about in Lexington where they got bars on the windows. Place looks like Dracula's castle."

"You can stay here. Live here."

"Where?"

"My house."

"Like that's gonna work." She slit her eyes at me.

"My mama . . . my parents . . . will let you and Kent live here."

"Why would they do that?"

"They will. My mama has always been real nice. She likes helping people."

"But your dad's back now. You don't know what he'll think. Besides, the law might not let them. Law might say me and Kent *have* to go to that orphanage. The walls are all stone and three feet thick, I hear."

"You and me can run away! We'll steal a boat tied up by the river and sail down to Cairo, Illinois, and then all the way down to New Orleans. I'll catch fish for us to eat. I'm real good at catching fish."

Kathy stared at me, frowning. "Who are you? Huckleberry Finn?"

"I'm serious." I saw us drifting down the Mississippi River with a big moon up in the sky, her leaning back against me in our boat.

"On a raft?"

"Speed boat."

"Do you know what the mosquitoes would be like? They'd eat us alive."

"Hey, you hungry?"

"No."

"You got to eat."

"I think I'm sick. I puked up that hotdog yesterday and the Dr Pepper."

"Must have been something wrong with those hotdogs. I saw lots of people puking."

She studied my face for a minute. "Not everybody. You didn't puke, did you?"

"Maybe some of the wieners were okay. Some not."

"*Did* you puke?"

"No."

"Did your mama?"

"No."

"Your sister?"

"No."

"But your daddy did."

"Did he? Yeah. So?"

"I did. Kent did, too."

"What you saying?"

"All us Dead people puked."

"You're not dead."

"I was. You know I was. Just like Kent and your daddy and Dr. Paul."

"That's impossible. And you don't look like them. They *look* dead. You don't. You look . . . real nice."

And all of a sudden she leaned down toward me from the rocking chair and kissed me. Her lips were warm and soft.

"You're real sweet," she said.

"You're beautiful."

"For a Dead girl."

"You're not dead. You're alive. And you're beautiful."

She had been looking into my eyes, but now she sat back and looked down at her hands in her lap.

"Yeah, especially when I'm pukin' my guts out." Her eyes connected with mine again. "I was dead. And I don't know what that means. Maybe I still am dead."

"I wouldn't care, even if you were."

"You wouldn't care if I was dead? You don't make a lot of sense." I leaned toward her this time, and we kissed again, only our lips touching. I wanted to kiss her all day, and I wanted to go someplace where I could put my hands on her and feel her hands on me. But I stopped myself and sat back down at her feet, and she leaned back in the rocker, and for a few seconds we were embarrassed, I guess, because we didn't look at each other. Instead, we inspected everything around the porch and the yard, the weeds and patches of dirt and old car corpses. The church songs sung by people who used to be dead floated from the front yard.

After a while, she gave me a little embarrassed smile. "Sorry I said that about your zits. You don't really have zits. Just a couple. Like three or four." She gazed at me, then away at nothing, then back at me. "Hey, I almost felt hungry for a second."

"See. You'll be okay."

*** 

I wanted to be with Kathy all the time. I liked the look

of her—her blonde eyebrows and eyelashes (which gave her face a soft look), the smooth whiteness of her neck, the fuzz at the base of her skull when she pulled her hair into two pony tails. I liked her thin body in her pale-green dress. She always wore dresses. In 1971, the county schools still didn't allow boys to have hair long enough to touch the collar of their shirt or girls to wear pants, only dresses and skirts that fell to the middle of the knee (or longer), and besides, girls and women who belonged to the FRG Church weren't allowed to wear anything but dresses, not even skirts. Her dress dipped in a modest crescent at her throat, and a small gold cross lay there against her skin. I liked the way her white socks started to droop and she kept pulling them up until I stole some fresh ones from Peggy's room. I had gotten her one of Peggy's dresses too but it was too big, so she put her own dress back on.

I liked her bare knees. She had a small white scar on her right kneecap, and I frequently imagined myself leaning down to it and kissing it, gently. I liked her long slim fingers, which made every gesture seem elegant. Her nails were short and, of course, unpainted. They were piano fingers, I thought, and I told her they were when she caught me staring at them and wanted to know what I was doing. She said she played an ancient pump organ at the Frog church. She played hymns but wished, she said, she could bust out some Chuck Berry rock 'n roll. She had no idea how to, though. She'd give anything if she could play Doors songs. I told her I played the guitar a little, so we could start a band. My sister did pretty good vocals. Peggy could do a fair imitation of Janis Joplin if her mood was silly or morose enough.

I liked Kathy's voice, which was soft and always a little husky like she had a cold. She smelled like flowers, and she smelled like the river, the good part—the smell of fresh water that you got when you were out on a boat in the middle of it and away from the shore and all the trash and dead fish.

I wanted to stay latched to her, never letting go of her hand, but I knew that being overly needy made people want to get away from you. I'd seen that work both ways with Peggy and her boyfriends. I knew there were times when Kathy wanted to be alone. She would become quiet and look away, out a window or at a lily on the wallpaper or at a cobweb on the sixteen-foot ceiling or, if we were outside, out across the blue Kentucky hills. I figured she might be thinking about her parents. She might even want to cry a while and not have me watching. So I would give her space. I'd wander off, and I knew she would find me when she wanted my company again, and I would maybe find a quiet place to be alone myself to think about what all had happened, what was happening, and what might happen.

*** 

This was not a movie, and I wasn't sure that the Dead were zombies, but I had seen zombie movies, and I'm not going to lie—I couldn't help thinking about them.

Mid-afternoon, while Kathy was off alone, I was in my room, lying on my bed, staring at the shelves of old leather books and wondering about people long dead writing them and people long dead reading them. I wondered if those nineteenth-century ancestors of mine ever imagined a future of cars and movies and airplanes and televisions and rocket ships that flew all the way to the moon. I was pretty sure they hadn't. I was sure they couldn't have, not any more than they could have imagined dead people walking out of the river.

And I thought again about The Dead appearing in the water, walking along the bottom of the river straight to shore, rising as the river bottom rose up to meet the land, me standing on the river bank and seeing the top of a head and then a forehead, a face, shoulders . . . . How could they breathe under water? Simple answer: they didn't. But they breathed now.

I fell asleep on my bed and The Dead kept rising, shedding sparkling water—about a dozen of them— and they came straight at me in my dream. They came closer and closer, and they were all chomping with big teeth like hungry cartoon dogs . . . .

Then I heard noises upstairs—bumps, thumps, creaks—that didn't sound like birds, and I was instantly up and running, though my head was stuffed full of dream fog. I took the stairs three at a time, hearing more noises—moans and grunts—and on an old love seat at the end of the second-floor hallway, Dr. Paul was on top of Peggy, eating her face.

I really thought he was eating her face.

I yelled, "Hey! Stop it!" and I rushed at him and grabbed him by his bony shoulders and threw him face down to the floor and got on his back with my arm around his throat so that I could choke him or break his neck or maybe tear his Goddamned head completely off.

Peggy was screaming behind me and I was relieved she was still alive, but then she grabbed me and pulled me off him, and I figured, *Oh my god, she has turned into a zombie too!*

She shoved me over onto the floor and was staring down at me, and she still had her face. It was all flushed and sweaty, but there weren't any chunks missing and there wasn't any blood. She was screaming at me, her mouth so wide I could see the cavities in her back teeth, and Dr. Paul got up and was rubbing his neck, his exposed brain flexing hard. Peggy kicked me in the side and then led Dr. Paul off into one of the bedrooms.

To their backs, I muttered, "Hey, I'm sorry."

***

Nan Mortimer had moved into our house that morning. Or at least onto our property. Scrappy little "Lois Lane" showed up with a portable manual typewriter, a camera, a backpack full of granola bars and canned beans, and a little tent that she pitched in the yard.

"I'm not asking for room and board," she said to my father and Mama and The Preacher on the front porch. "I'm a self-sufficient observer of these miraculous events."

My parents, who were holding hands, smiled and nodded. "Plenty of room," they said in unison.

The Preacher put his arm around her shoulders and said she was welcome to observe. "We need a chronicler of these days. I ask nothing of you, Miss Mortimer, but objective reporting."

"The only kind of reporting I know how to do."

As soon The Preacher and Mama and my father went back into the house, she looked at me and Kathy sitting on the old scuffed-up and chewed-up church pew that had been on the porch my whole life and said, "Hey, kiddos, I got lots of questions for you. Don't stray off too far."

"You doing another story for the Portsmouth paper?" I asked.

"Hell no. I quit that crap newspaper. Twenty years of their crap. Bastards didn't even believe me when I gave them my Fourth of July story. They wouldn't run it! Said I needed to take off a week and see a shrink."

"Well, you can kind of understand . . . "

"I don't give a good shit. I'm writing a book about all this incredible stuff happening!"

She actually didn't look like Lois Lane anymore because she had shed her 1950s suit and high heels for cut-off jeans, sneakers, and a Cincinnati Reds tee-shirt. It was weird seeing her dressed so differently and seeing the wildness in her eyes and hearing her cuss. She was like another person.

Throughout the day she did interviews with people whose loved ones had returned and with some of The Dead, but she found that most of The Dead didn't have much to say. She snapped photographs. In between interviews, she sat on the porch Indian style with the little typewriter at her feet and tapped furiously, her fingers just flying, the little bell on the typewriter going *ding!* every few seconds and her saying "shit" for every typo.

She kept asking me questions. "What all did you observe when that preacher guy stood in the river calling on God to undo the bus accident?"

"I don't know. There was a lot of glare from the sun."

We were sitting on the front porch on that old church pew, which according to family legend came from an abandoned Quaker settlement around 1900 and had been carried home in the back of my grandpa's wagon.

"Was he naked when he was standing in the river?"

"No. He had a black suit on. He looked like a regular preacher."

"How long you think his penis is?"

"What?"

She shook her head fast. "Never mind. . . . So how does it make you feel to have a house full of zombies?"

Several Dead men had just pulled up in the hog truck with a load of lumber. They jumped out and started unloading two-by-eights and one-by-six deck boards. They moved around with the agility of healthy men. I asked Miss Mortimer, "What makes you think they're zombies?"

"They look like zombies."

"The Preacher says they're resurrected folks. He says God gave him the power to resurrect."

"Okay, The Resurrected. What's it like having them around?"

"They seem nice enough."

"Your dad's obviously one of the zom — Resurrected."

"Yeah, so?"

"Has he said anything about talking to God or living in Heaven or anything like that?"

"He says he doesn't remember anything."

"Has your girlfriend changed?"

"What do you mean?"

"Since the accident. Her behavior? Her attitude? Her interests?" Jan gave me a little smile all of a sudden and a nudge with her elbow. "The way she kisses?"

"I . . . I didn't know her real good before."

"What's it like having a zombie girlfriend?"

"She's not—"

"Right. Resurrected."

"Zombies want to eat people, don't they? Kathy isn't trying to eat anybody."

"Right, right. Resurrected."

"She's not hungry at all. I can't get her eat."

"Well, a girl's got to keep her figure," Nan said, batting her eyelashes.

***

At first, Dr. Paul had the idea that he would finish his trip to Cincinnati. He insisted that he could simply walk into Mercy Hospital and announce he was ready to begin doctoring, just 48 years later than expected. Surely, they could find paperwork about his hiring, he speculated.

Peggy used what little mental power she had to persuade him that no one would know who he was and that he would likely end up as a patient in the psych ward.

His exposed brain tissue flushed purple and pulsated quickly. She then had an easy time persuading him to make Devil's Elbow his home. The town had never had a doctor. To have one in residence would be a true sign of progress and a great benefit to Elbowers, she told him.

Dr. Paul's exposed brain latched onto the idea pretty quickly, and immediately, with the help of "Nurse Peggy," he set up a medical clinic in the front parlor and the connecting den of our house. Peggy said it was the perfect location for an office because people could watch *The Price Is Right* and *The Newlywed Game* and all the soap operas in the den while they waited to see the good doctor.

By early afternoon, Dr. Paul had a dozen people waiting. It helped that he put out word that a physical exam was fifty cents and that surgical procedures would run anywhere between one and five dollars. These were reasonable prices in 1923. People—Living and Dead—with aches and pains they'd been coping with for months or years showed up to be healed.

Nan Mortimer interviewed waiting patients. "So you think a dead doctor can help you? You know, I think his license to practice medicine might be expired." After they were examined, she'd ask, "How'd it go?"

An elderly Living woman said, "He lanced an old boil I had like cutting butter. He has a gentle way. I don't give two hoots if he's dead or alive. And he charged me only seventy-five cents."

He looked down people's throats and tapped their knees with a rubber mallet Peggy found in the barn and peered into their ears with a flashlight and thumped on their backs and took their pulses. He examined The Dead and declared them all healthy. He looked into my father's vacant bloody eye sockets and said he was fine. He looked into the hole where an ear should be, down the throat of a person without a jaw, and said, "Excellent. You're healthy as a horse."

The living, on the other hand, had all kinds of things wrong with them, he explained to each somberly. He said Mama had iron-poor blood. Most of the Living had more serious conditions. There were signs of heart disease, cancer, rickets, shingles, hernia, urinary-tract infections, psoriasis, eczema, syphilis, gonorrhea, ringworm, gout, hepatitis, hardening of the arteries . . . .

He prescribed mustard plasters and lots of castor

oil, hot tea, cold coffee, and long walks.

While Dr. Paul examined patients throughout the afternoon, music filled the house. In the music room, one of The Dead played our antique piano with her elegantly long fingers bereft of flesh as beautifully as an out-of-tune piano can be played. Classical tunes—Mozart, Beethoven, Chopin—and some 1940s show tunes. There was more music out in the front yard. The Dead—mostly older ladies and a few older men—sang solemn hymns and raucous gospel. The only kid in the choir was Kathy's brother, Kent. He had a really nice high voice. Kathy said he was as good as Michael Jackson of the Jackson Five, and I agreed. The Preacher declared all the members of his choir to be angels come back from the dead to help prepare the world for the End of Days.

The more youthful and randy sought to create a music of their own. A Dead teenage boy sped recklessly past the house in The Preacher's Buick Riviera, The Rolling Stones blaring from the radio—"Can't Get No Satisfaction!" A Dead girl was nearly in the boy's lap, the two of them in a serious lip lock. A few hundred feet down the road they crashed into a tree. They were okay, though. They just climbed out and started making out on the crumpled hood, steam rising from the cracked radiator.

Couples—two Dead or one Dead and one Living—slinked off to outbuildings or hid behind trees or bushes. The young Living and Dead seemed to possess a voracious appetite for each other's flesh, and their heavy breathing and guttural moans and high-pitched gasps and screams of pleasure wafted across the hills above the Ohio River and blended with the hymns and the piano music.

*\*\**

In the evening, as the sun was setting blood red between two dark hills, The Preacher was on the side porch making plans with twelve Dead men who sat at his feet as he stood above them. He said that as soon as Mr. Lloyd, his recently returned son, and my dad overhauled the engine, replaced the brakes, and got some new or newer tires on the hog truck, they would all embark on a road trip, first to the steps of the state capitol building in Frankfort and then on to Lexington and Louisville, to show themselves to the world and save as many souls as they could and generally prepare righteous Christians for The Glorious End of Times.

"We are saviors! You and you and you. And me. Saviors. Thus we must save!"

And The Dead nodded their smashed skulls, waved their arm or arms (if they had both) in the air, and raised their empty eye sockets to the porch ceiling, which Miss Trout had explained to me was painted sky blue to ward off flies, wasps, and demons. "No de-man," she had said, "can walk cross a blue porch and get in nobody's house."

I noticed Miss Trout sitting on her own porch across the road, and I was wondering if she was saying something I couldn't hear because it looked like her mouth was open. I was about to head over to see if she needed something, but just then a '61 white Chrysler Imperial clattered into the yard, seemingly out of nowhere.

In it were two men in their dark Sunday suits, their faces red and sweaty. The car pulled up about twenty feet from the porch and turned around to face the road like they wanted to be able to get away quickly.

The men made no move to get out of the car, but the driver made a gesture that wasn't exactly a wave, more just a flick of his wrist, and said in a soft, gravelly voice, "Preacher, we need to talk." The driver didn't turn the car off. It idled roughly, trembling like somebody consumed by fever or rage, and black smoke spewed from the tailpipe. The exhaust fumes filled the yard and burned my eyes.

The Preacher turned to his twelve and said they'd continue planning later. The Dead men meandered off toward the front yard. The men in the Imperial watched The Dead with sneers on their red faces. The passenger spit tobacco juice out his window.

The Preacher turned back to the men in the Chrysler and squinted at them. "Evenin,' brothers. How might I help you?"

The driver said in his gravelly voice, louder this time, "We had us a meetin' at the F.R.G. this evenin' and we come to the conclusion that what has happened is no less than a devil-inspired abomination."

The Preacher looked off at the setting sun and said, "I appreciate a man that doesn't mince words."

"Then you'll 'preciate the fact that we got to send these demons back to hell."

The Preacher, his eyes full of the sun, looked at the man. "Say what, friend?" He stepped off the porch, and I could tell by the men's eyes that they saw him naked. They were watching his big cock swing as he approached their car, and the man in the passenger seat pulled up a sawed-off shotgun from between his legs and pointed it at The Preacher.

"Don't get no closer." The man's face had gone from red to purple. He had a salt-and-pepper crew cut, and I recognized him now as a farmer. He had a lot of chickens, and Mama bought fresh eggs from him.

The Preacher stopped. "You say you're from the F.R.G. Church? My friends, half your congregation has visited here today to celebrate this *miracle*." He threw his arms wide. "Some are here right now round front and inside. They're havin' picnics with returned loved ones. Eatin' fried chicken and catfish and prayin' and singin' hymns."

"They ain't members of our church no more. They done joined league with the Devil," the driver said. He had a hat on, the kind businessmen used to wear all the time, and sunglasses.

"The Devil?" The Preacher frowned. "Are you saying I'm the Devil? These fine men you just saw here? That boy there?" And he pointed at me.

The two men glared at me. They squinted their mean eyes at me like they'd just as soon shoot me or hang me from a tree as look at me.

"Ain't nothin' natural 'bout any of this. This is the work of Satan."

"Friends, this is the work of God —"

When the driver spoke this time, split flew from his mouth. "Where's my little Julie then?"

And I realized who he was. Mr. Martens. He was a shift supervisor at the feed mill over near Pig Gut. He had a daughter who died of Leukemia the year before.

"Friend, I can't explain the choices of the Good Lord—"

"Stop callin' me 'friend.' I ain't your friend," Mr. Martens said. The way his voice broke I thought he might start crying. "Dwayne here is my friend and an obedient servant of the lord, and what he would like to do better than anything right now is blow your damned head off. But some of us think you and your Devil's freak show ought be given a chance to just get on out of here and go far away. Mostly, people are worried 'bout the law comin' in if we take matters in our own hands. So as long as you go away far, we don't care. Maybe go to Canada. We're tryin' to be Christ-like 'bout this."

Dwayne kept his shotgun pointed at The Preacher, but turned his head and spit tobacco juice out the passenger window again. I remembered then that his last name was Hickman and that I had heard he used to have a son, but the son had gotten killed in a tractor or hay-baler accident.

Mr. Hickman looked at The Preacher again and spoke: "Sundown by tomorrow night you and all these freak devils be gone, or we ain't bein' so Christ-like no more. We're gonna cleanse the earth of ya. Law or no law, fire will rain down."

Mr. Martens stepped on the gas and the Imperial shot out of the yard.

The Preacher and I watched the road after they were long gone, black exhaust swirling in the air like they had left ghosts of themselves behind. Finally, The Preacher looked at me and said, "I seen their kind before. Full of sorrow and confusion and hate for what they can't have or don't understand. They'll come round."

He walked away toward the front of the house and started hollering, "Fellowship time! Let's do some testifying! Gather round, my flock! Gather round!"

I noticed that Miss Trout still seemed to be trying to say something across the road in the twilight, her mouth wide open, and I started her way again, but this time I felt a cool hand on my arm. It was Kathy, and she was grinning at me, and she said, "Let's go somewhere."

***

Not all of The Dead were interested in the fellowship services or testifying. The ones making love behind bushes or in the woods certainly weren't. Some just wanted to get back to their lives, lives they had missed out on for five or ten or twenty or thirty or more years. They had no interest in becoming members of what The Preacher had dubbed The Church of the Arisen Righteous Saviors or CARS.

Kathy and I went to my room and barricaded the door with stacks of old books (the door lock had been broken for probably half a century). For a while, we sat on the edge of my bed and looked out through the thick, wavy nineteenth-century window glass at the darkening side yard, lone Dead people milling about, looking lost or reflective or anxious. Occasionally couples came back from their secret places, holding hands. Beyond the yard, in the distance, was the twinkle of the Ohio River and the black silhouette of the Ohio hills.

Every once in a while, Kathy and I would glance at each other. The room was almost black. Kathy asked me to light a candle, and I put it on the bedside table next to us.

When a couple—a middle-aged Living woman and a slim young Dead man—passed close to the window, Kathy reached over and took my hand. We continued to look out the window, not talking, but occasionally we stole glances at each other. Finally, we turned and gazed at each other. Then we kissed. Then we touched each other. Then we talked. A lot.

Things moved fast, the way they often do when you're sixteen. We planned a whole lifetime in the course of the night.

We talked about getting jobs in Maysville (she could waitress and I could work in a mill) so that we could get a trailer to live in, one with a spare bedroom so that her brother could live with us. We could get married. Plenty of kids in Kentucky got married when they were sixteen.

And we talked about things that worried us.

"Have you slept?" I asked.

She shrugged. "I don't think so. Sometimes I kind of zone out."

"But you haven't slept?"

"No."

"You tired?"

"No."

I nodded. "You eat anything yet?"

"No."

"Not in three days?"

"No."

"You hungry?"

"No."

"Not at all?"

"I don't think so."

It was black in my room. I couldn't see her. Outside, the sky was full of stars and the moon was full.

# DAY FOUR

*The Hunger*

The weather turned cool the next day, and clouds formed in the sky. Throughout the morning, the temperature dropped instead of rising. The thermometer on the front porch read sixty-five degrees, then sixty, then fifty-five. The clouds were thick and dark. It was hard to believe—hard to remember—that it had been over a hundred degrees on July Fourth, just two days before.

Goose bumps covered my arms when I stepped out onto the porch mid-morning, groggy from a night of no sleep. I was inspecting the sky when I noticed that Miss Trout was still sitting in her rocker across the road, seemingly trying to tell me something, but she was leaning stiffly and far to the right now, and I knew without going across the road that she was dead.

The Preacher and several Dead men were building a stage in the yard. The sounds of sawing and hammering echoed across the hills. The Preacher was hand sawing a board, making long, fast cuts. When I told him about Miss Trout, he frowned, but only for a moment, and then his eyes lit up. "Time to try some new style resurrectin', boy!" he said with enthusiasm.

I watched as he and a couple of Dead women hustled across the road. The women straightened Miss Trout in her chair, and The Preacher flapped his arms kind of like a big chicken or turkey and began speaking in tongues. He got louder and louder until finally all The Dead stopped what they were doing and stood and watched. The two Dead women, one on each side of the corpse, prayed loudly, their eyes squeezed shut, while The Preacher waved his bible and jabbered away. The cheeks of his ass puckered tight together when his words became emphatic.

But Miss Trout did not stir.

God did not act.

Dr. Paul came out of my house, and he went across the road and stood on the porch step but just watched. Peggy came out of the house and stood next to me. She had big hickeys and teeth marks all over her neck and face.

"Jesus," I said. "What happened to you?"

"I have no idea what you're talkin' about."

"You know what."

"Well, what do you think? Paul looks pretty meek, but he's a real animal when he gets goin'." She grinned big enough that I could see where she was missing her canine tooth on her left side.

"Looks like your face hurts."

"It's good pain."

The Preacher suddenly wailed and fell to his knees on Miss Trout's porch. There was a snap of old pine wood or old bone

I couldn't tell which. Miss Trout had slumped back to the right side.

Dr. Paul put his hand on The Preacher's shoulder, as The Preacher began to sob.

The Dead slowly went back to building the stage. Nobody talked for a while.

***

When The Preacher came back to the house, he walked straight over to me on the porch and said, "What say you, boy?"

I looked at him a minute, puzzled, shaking my head, waiting. Finally, I asked, "Say 'bout what?"

He waved an arm toward Miss Trout's shack. "It was your idea for me to raise her."

"All I did was tell you she was . . . gone."

He sighed, looked up at the black sky and then

back at me. "Yeah, she's gone. *Gone* gone. The good lord doesn't want her back here. Maybe because of her voodoo. Maybe I've been trying to summon her from Heaven but she's in Hell."

"Maybe it's cause she didn't die in the river."

"I know that, boy!"

"Well, then—"

"I was hoping . . . ." After he trailed off, he just looked down at his bare feet for a while. Or maybe he was looking at his pecker.

The Dead were all silent. They looked at each other sideways. They whispered if they spoke at all. They were troubled too by The Preacher's failure to resurrect Miss Trout.

"Somebody should bury her," I said.

His head snapped up. "That's it. Come with me, boy!"

He hustled back across the road, not paying any attention to a 1951 Hudson Hornet roaring toward him, honking madly and almost splattering him to Kingdom Come. Seven or eight men were squeezed into the Hudson, and the car skidded to a stop, and the men stuck guns out the windows. "You gonna die, Devil!" one of the men shouted and fired off a round from his rifle into the sky. Then they roared off.

"Pay those fools no mind, boy," The Preacher said as the gunshot echoed across the hills.

On Miss Trout's porch, The Preacher said, "Take her feet." He grabbed her shoulders. She was light. It was like picking up a hollowed-out log. We carried her over to the hog truck, laid her in the bed, and The Preacher said, "Keys in it. You drive."

"I don't know I can. Not this thing."

"All things are possible with help of the lord."

It occurred to me that he probably couldn't work the truck's pedals with his bare feet. If he thought he was wearing golden robes, what did he think he had on his feet?

The Preacher hopped into the passenger seat. I had to slam the driver's door three times before it latched. The bench seat belched rotted padding. The windshield was divided into two pieces, and the passenger piece was cracked across its entire length. My hands sweated and shook as I fumbled to turn the ignition key.

The monster lurched forward violently. The Preacher slammed into the dash. Miss Trout slid and cracked the top of her head into the cab.

"Good Christ, boy! Take it out of gear!"

"Jesus! Sorry."

I took a few breaths.

Then I got it in neutral and tried again.

I hadn't driven much—Mama's Mercury Comet a few times but it had an automatic transmission, and I was having a hell of a time with the stiff gearshift and sticky clutch of the old hog hauler.

I took it easy down the mountain, pumping the brakes, which screeched like cats in heat. We moved at a whining, roaring, creaking crawl. I thought I heard The Preacher mutter, "Jesus Christ on a cross."

When we approached the overhang on Devil's Elbow Road, he shouted, "Stop! Stop!"

I was still bringing the truck to an easy, screeching stop, when The Preacher jumped out. He reached into the bed, hauled out Miss Trout and hustled to the edge of the cliff with her on the back of his shoulders. With no words that I heard and with no hesitation, he pressed her above his head like a weightlifter and flung her over the cliff.

I gasped. "What you do that for?"

He turned back to me. "You comin' down or goin' home? I can walk. Faster if I walk, the way *you* drive."

I stared at his gray chest hair and moles on his belly. I had a feeling The Preacher was just in for more disappointment, and besides, I wanted to get back to

Kathy.

"I gotta get back," I said.

"Good luck, boy." He started away, then stopped, and when he looked back, his eyes were sympathetic. "I ain't sayin' that truck's easy. You pray all the way back, and I'll pray for you. You make it in one piece, and you can call yourself a man."

As he marched away again, he raised his fist in the air. "I shall return, boy!"

I drove all the way back in second gear, trembling in terror that the truck was going to stall and then start rolling backwards and the brakes wouldn't hold. Maybe because I was breathing so hard, I became more aware of how bad the truck smelled—a combination of old cigarette smoke, gasoline, and pig manure.

When I arrived home (and, yes, I was quick to thank God), I was exhausted and covered in sweat despite the cool temperature. I was soaked like I'd been dunked in the river.

The door of Miss Trout's shack stood open, and it was strange and creepy to think how she would never be there again after she had been there every day of her ninety-five years.

\*\*\*

There was the strangeness and creepiness of that empty shack across the road, but there was something else, too. A dark mood was spreading among The Dead.

As the men built their stage, they snapped at each other—"You dumb bastard!" and at inanimate objects: "Damn saw." They became awkward and jerky in their movements. They slammed their thumbs while trying to drive nails. They sawed into their thighs. They cut boards too short. They dropped lumber on their toes or on others' toes. They looked up at the dark sky a lot. They clutched their stomachs.

The women tried to sew and wash their ragged clothes in wash tubs in the yard and became confused when the cloth disintegrated in their hands. "What in the world . . . ?" Then they broke down and cried, clutching what had become rags.

Lovers sat silently and apart now.

The Dead kept clutching their stomachs and then they started groaning in pain.

Dr. Paul and Peggy walked through the house and all around the porches and the yard, passing out saltine crackers and slices of Wonder Bread. "Chew it slowly," Dr. Paul said and patted shoulders.

Nan Mortimer offered her granola bars and canned beans to get The Dead to talk to her, but The Dead were in no mood for interviews.

The Dead turned up their noses at all the food offered. A few took small bites, but most spit the bread or the crackers out immediately. They threw the bean cans at Miss Mortimer.

They weren't eating and they weren't talking.

Dr. Paul kept telling them all, "Go on. We've got to eat." He ate a little of the soft white Wonder Bread himself.

Mama was trying to get my father to eat, and he suddenly exploded, "Get the hell away from me, woman. Jesus Christ, is this what I came back for? To be nagged to death? Go the hell away!"

Mama ran off to her room in tears.

Some of the Dead kept trying to eat. They took small bites, chewing slowly, swallowing with effort, throats bulging.

Then they smiled. Briefly.

A Dead woman in a black dress and with her gray hair pulled back into a bun on her busted skull raised her arms. In a weak, crackling voice, she said, "Praise . . . Jesus!" Then she puked.

They all puked.

Dr. Paul and all the rest of them.

Kathy puked, and I rubbed her back until she stopped and stood up straight. I thought I was going to cry, but I forced myself not to.

They puked white mush.

And in the middle of this puke fest, The Preacher came trudging into the yard with Miss Trout's sopping wet corpse flung over his shoulder. In the middle of the yard, he rolled her gently off his back and laid her on the ground.

He stared down at her for a minute, and then, his head hanging morosely, The Preacher walked off, disappearing into the woods.

Several of The Dead gathered around Miss Trout's body, seeming very curious. Their nostrils flared. They bared their teeth.

I said to Kathy, "They act like they've never seen a dead person before."

\*\*\*

When The Preacher returned from the woods, it was downright chilly, and his skin was puckered and his privates had shriveled up to almost nothing. But his face shone like he'd found a place where the sun was shining and he had stared into it a good part of the afternoon. He walked with purpose, his shoulders thrown back. He said to me and Kathy on the front porch, "Everything is going to be okay." He looked around. "Where's Miss Trout?"

I realized for the first time that her body was gone. "I don't know. I guess somebody buried her."

Just then, we all heard two howls like a couple of The Dead had reclaimed the horniness of the day before.

***

As night approached, the clouds dissipated and the sky became a crisp dark blue, and the sun and moon appeared simultaneously. The mercury in the thermometer on the porch post showed thirty-three degrees. Thirty-three degrees in July.

And all The Dead who had risen from the river gathered in my front yard, not just the ones who had nowhere else to go and had been with us all along but also the ones who had been reunited and gone home with loved ones. Mr. Davis' mother came. Mr. Lloyd's son. The Frog preacher's daughter. Most showed up on foot, but some drove. A Dead lady with empty eye sockets drove up into the yard in a yellow VW Beetle with its high beams on and parked neatly off to the side. By this time, the idea of an eyeless corpse driving and being able to see didn't surprise me. Corpses walked on broken legs, lifted lumber and swung hammers with broken arms, talked with brains oozing down the back of their neck.

I don't know what exactly pulled them to my house, whether The Preacher or someone else made phone calls or sent out messengers or whether there was some mystical *Star Trek*-like tractor beam pulling them in against their will, but they came.

And they were all hungry, clutching their stomachs, some of them puking up food they'd tried to eat—hamburgers, chili dogs, mashed potatoes, grits, apples, tomatoes, corn bread . . .

They puked and moaned and shivered in the July cold.

***

The Preacher stood on the four-foot-high, twelve-foot-by-twelve-foot stage they had built in the front yard, and he surveyed his flock of Dead. His naked flesh puckered against the cold, and his dark eyes caught the last rays of sunlight clinging to the horizon. The Dead were restive, standing below him. They twitched and jerked and let out strange sounds, like the special-education kids at my school, who were isolated in their own classroom in the basement under the building's pipes. If you sat in a classroom near the heater vent, you'd sometimes hear clanging noises, moans, shouts, screams, and unworldly jabbering coming up from that underground room that no regular kid ever saw.

The Preacher studied the restless Dead. Every once in a while, his eyes lifted, peered above the heads of The Dead and landed on me and Kathy. We stood on the side porch of the house. I had put on a winter coat. I could hear Nan Mortimer dictating softly into her tape recorder, describing the gathering. She had on long jeans now and a sweat shirt and a wool cap. Kathy still wore her pale-green dress and insisted she wasn't cold, although I could see the goose bumps on her slim arms, and her lips looked gray.

The Preacher leaned his head to one side and then the other. His head rocked back and forth like a metronome for a good five minutes, his lips pursed, his brow furrowed.

Then he paced the stage, from edge to edge, corner to corner. Twelve feet one way, twelve feet another. The Dead stood on all four sides of him. When he started talking, it was in a strange tongue. He seemed to be talking just to himself because his chin rested on his chest, his eyes on the ground, on which frost had started to form. Everything—the grass, the stage, the old car corpses, Dead people's hair—was turning white.

His pacing got faster and faster, until I thought he was going to break into a run, and his strange words came faster and faster, too. His feet left footprints in the frost that had formed on his stage.

The Dead watched The Preacher as they twitched and groaned, occasionally letting out a swear word. A boy in denim coveralls near the stage said with some real conviction, "Pig crap!"

Some had started to sneer, and others were grinding their teeth.

A bent old lady in the back of the gathering said flatly, "Cocksucker."

The Preacher halted.

Then he approached the boy in coveralls and said something to him in a soft voice. The boy nodded and reached into a pocket and handed The Preacher a Swiss Army knife.

The Preacher faced his Dead and said, "Eat of my flesh and drink of my blood so that you may have eternal life!"

The Dead instantly stopped their twitching and moaning. They stood stock still and silent.

The Preacher opened the large blade of the pocket knife and swiftly sliced into his forearm, did some skillful and rapid cutting like he was a master of Thanksgiving-turkey carving, and before I fully registered in my brain what was happening, he dangled a little chunk of his flesh before them. Blood streamed down his arm, across the back of his hand, and dripped onto the frosted-over pine decking he stood on.

Nan Mortimer's voice rose an octave as she described to her tape recorder what was happening.

"Come, little brother," The Preacher said, smiling and nodding, and the crowd parted to let a little boy approach. The Preacher reached down and picked up the boy and placed him on the stage.

"Open your mouth and eat of my flesh."

The Preacher popped the little chunk of his forearm into the little boy's mouth like a wafer.

The Dead all stared, frozen and silent.

The boy closed his eyes and chewed. We were all mesmerized by the working of the muscles in his jaw. Then he swallowed, and we watched the flexing of his throat. Kathy squeezed my hand harder and harder as all this was happening.

Finally, she screamed, "Kent!"

And only then did it really register in my brain that the boy on the stage was Kathy's brother.

"Kent!"

Kathy started toward the stage, but I held her back. She twisted and swung her elbows. One elbow caught me just below my eye, but I held tight.

I heard Mama scream from the front porch. Then she yelled, "Peggy!" And the screen on the front door slammed. The latch clicked.

Kathy stopped trying to get away, but held my hand and dug her fingernails into my palm to the point of drawing blood.

"Darling, come here," said The Preacher to a young woman, who had probably been pretty when she was alive but now had an open and continuously pulsating gash straight from the corner of her right eye to the tip of her chin. "That's right, sister. Step on up to the edge of this stage. Right here." She did and he stood above her and reached his bloody arm toward her and said, "Drink of my blood, and you shall drink of life." And she began licking the back of his hand. She licked faster and faster and started making slurping noises. Then she reached up and turned his hand over and, with her long pink tongue, licked his palm sensuously. The Preacher looked up at the cold sky filling with bright stars, and he grinned like a sailor in a whore house, and when she took his little finger into her mouth and bit it off in one swift bite, he shouted, "Hallelujah!"

Nan Mortimer started screaming—a blood-curdling soprano screech.

And The Dead all moved as one. A wave of Dead swept upon the stage with a unified roar of hunger, and The Preacher vanished in the midst of them. I heard him shout "Hallelujah!" three more times, in rapid succession. Then his voice was silenced. The stage throbbed and sounded like a big bass drum. No one was shouting Hallelujah. There were plenty of sounds, though—smacking, chomping, slurping, stomping, moaning, tearing.

But no one said Hallelujah.

Nan Mortimer kept screaming. If a woman's scream was capable of breaking glass, her scream would have done it.

Then there was the sound of bones snapping. I recognized the sound from my dogs eating chicken bones and from being at a football game the autumn before where the quarterback from our high school got hit from the side by a beefy lineman and everybody in the bleachers on both sides of the field could hear his femur snap.

The Dead were like a bunch of football players who had piled on the guy with the ball. As the moaning and other sounds started to subside, the boy in the coveralls who had given The Preacher his pocket knife straightened up from the pile, and his head swiveled until his blood-smeared face came around at me, and he stared at me across my yard, and then he lifted his nose like he was catching a scent. When he lowered his face, he stood up, separating himself from the others. He stepped down from the stage and took two steps toward me and Kathy, his eyes focused on me.

Nan Mortimer was still screaming, and I guess her tape recorder got it all.

***

Then a shotgun exploded. It shook the earth like a lightning strike or a big tree falling. Sulfur wafted over the chaos. The boy in the coveralls took two more steps toward us, but his shoulders were jerking and half his head was gone. Another blast and he didn't have a head at all and fell like a sack of chicken feed.

Moving across the yard from the road was a posse of Frogs armed with rifles, pistols, pitchforks, lengths of galvanized water pipe, and self-righteousness. Their furious faces gleamed with sweat in the chilly night.

I looked at Kathy, and she was staring at the scene with no expression on her face, a blank dazed look. I was working my jaw trying to get words out. She took a step forward, as if toward the stage to join the pile-on, and she muttered, "Kent," but I grabbed her arm.

Another explosion. Then a whole volley of gunshots. The Frogs kept coming closer. Blood smeared and with strips of flesh hanging from their teeth, The Dead stood from their pile-on of The Preacher, or what was left of him, and they twisted to see what the commotion was.

I knew that Kathy and I needed to be running, but for the moment I was hypnotized by the melee.

Heads exploded in clouds of blood, bone, and brain. Dead people aren't dumb. They knew they needed to take evasive action. They dropped to the ground or crouched behind the four-foot-high stage. When the Frogs came at them with the pitchforks and the pipes, The Dead fought back. They grabbed the weapons away from their attackers—and used them not so much with skill but without reservation and with ferocity.

The Dead let out no screams, but the Frogs did. "Jezzzzusssss!"

The Dead, though, made the mistake of taking time to eat their victims, giving other Frogs a chance to come up on them with a pipe or to take aim with a gun.

The Dead were dying again. Mr. Davis' mother got a pitchfork through her face. Mr. Lloyd's son got an axe driven deep into the back of his skull. I had a feeling that this time they wouldn't be coming back.

Maybe a minute had passed. That's all.

"We got to get inside!" I shouted at Kathy.

What little bit of my brain that was working told me safety was in my house. After all, it was my home. I could shut the windows. I could lock the doors. It was my home. When I was little, Mama would ask me whether everybody in kindergarten or first grade was being nice to me, and when I'd nod, she'd say, "They better. I'd hate to have to start kickin' butts. Nobody's allowed to be mean to my baby."

For a split second, my fantasy was to be a little kid again, with nothing to worry about except what was for supper and whether Santa Claus would bring me a GI Joe. But I had no time for fantasy. I tugged

Kathy's arm.

She had lost the blank daze and looked at me, her eyes wide, confused, frightened.

I tugged her arm again. At first, I was dragging her, it seemed, but by the time we got around to the front porch she was right behind me, her breath on my neck, and we witnessed Nan Mortimer's screams silenced by a Dead teenage girl, who tore out half of Nan's throat in one violent chomp. The girl looked at us and spoke with her mouth full: "I couldn't take any more of that bitch's screaming."

The screen door was hanging by one hinge. The inside door was open. As we crossed the threshold into the only home I'd ever known, I recognized Mr. Martens' voice behind us. "Get her, men!"

I knew he meant Kathy.

I slammed the door behind us and turned the lock.

We ran. Vaguely, as soon as we were in the house, I was aware of a smacking, slurping sound, and as we passed the front parlor I got a glimpse of my mama sprawled limply on her back, her torso torn open and my father kneeling beside her on the floor, pulling her intestines out like a string of bloody sausages.

Then we were on the stairs, the risers creaking loudly, Kathy's hand gripping mine so hard it hurt.

On the second-floor landing, we raced down the hallway for the attic door, and two things happened at once—I heard the explosion of wood and glass (the front door) and we passed the old master bedroom and through the open doorway I saw Dr. Paul tearing off my sister's nose with his teeth.

Then we were at the attic door, and I pulled the door knob.

The Frogs were in the house. A shotgun exploded and I imagined my father's head disintegrating. Someone shouted, "Unholy bastards!" in that thick hillbilly tone that was somehow distinct to residents of Devil's Elbow, a certain half note in the screech of the last syllable of "unholeeeee!"

For whatever reason, I expected that attic door to be stuck or locked, but it flew open and I fell back against Kathy, and we both went sprawling. I knocked my head on the wall and was seeing stars, but I got on my feet right away, reached down and swiped at Kathy's blurry hand, missed it, swiped again, connected, and pulled her up. We staggered into the stairwell. I pulled the door closed gently and flipped the ancient catch on the lock. As we flew up the attic steps, there was another shotgun blast—for Dr. Paul, I assumed.

At the top of the stairs, I held Kathy, who was trembling now. I said, "It's going to be okay."

She pulled away from me gently and looked at me. There was no fear in her face, no tears in her eyes. "I feel strange," she said.

"Strange how?"

"I . . . I don't know." Then there *was* fear in her face, and she crumpled to the floor and covered her face with her hands. She said something I couldn't understand.

"What?"

"Go away."

"Why?"

"I'm starting to feel . . . hungry." She was turned away from me, her face buried between her knees. "Leave. Now."

"No. You're not like them."

"How do you know?"

Another shotgun blast on the second floor. Kathy jumped. "They're going to . . . kill me."

"No, they're not. You're not Dead. You're beautiful."

"I haven't eaten . . . ."

"It doesn't matter. I love you. You love me. Look at me. I want to see your face."

"They're going to kill me."

"I won't let them. Look at me."

"What if I *kill you*?"

"You won't."

"Why not?"

"Because you're not like them. You're not one of them . . . . One of the Dead. Now look at me."

She raised her head slowly, and she turned toward me. I pulled her toward a round window where cool moonlight streamed in. A scream from the first floor sounded, a man's scream, and the scream went on and on, and then there was a gunshot, a .22 rifle maybe. Kathy didn't flinch this time. And everything was quiet except for the echo in my ears. The smell of sulfur wafted up through the floor.

Then she was facing me, and the light from the round window shone on her face, and she looked the way she always looked. She hadn't changed.

"See," I said. "You're not hungry."

"I can't hurt you. I won't let myself." She shivered. "But I *am* hungry."

Footsteps pounded below.

"Look in the attic!" someone hollered.

They started pounding on the attic door. It wouldn't keep them out long.

Without emotion, Kathy said, "They'll kill us both."

Our eyes met, and I nodded. I swung the round window open on its hinge. It wasn't a big window, but we were both thin and we could squeeze through it. "Hurry. We'll jump to the porch roof."

"It's too far."

"No." The wood of the attic door started cracking and splintering, and we heard the grunting of the men breaking it.

"Too far," she said again. But she was beside me at the window. Footsteps sounded on the attic steps.

"No!" And I pushed her and she squeezed through and fell, and I was right behind her.

There was no sensation of flying, just the sudden terror of falling, of having no control, and then instantly hitting the rough tar roofing, feeling and hearing my arm snap, my vision going red, my ears roaring so loud I could no longer hear anything else.

Kathy pulled me up and she made me start sliding down a column, my legs and my one good arm wrapped around it. I fell half way down the column and landed on my tailbone on the wooden porch and an electric shock went up my spine. I fell back and knocked the back of my head, and lay flat, and everything went from red to black but only for a few seconds because Kathy was tugging on my good arm, and I found myself getting to my feet and stumbling after her across the side yard—running, falling, getting up, running—into the woods.

Then the roar in my ears faded, and I heard the Frogs shouting, coming, the rustle of high grass and the breaking of twigs and trampling of bushes.

Kathy said nothing. I said nothing. The cold air lit up my sweat and my pain, and I trembled as I ran.

Every few seconds I glimpsed Devil's Elbow Road through the trees. Then Kathy veered away from the road and we were on a steep decline that led to the river, and we slid and fell and rolled and caught ourselves and then slid some more. I bit my lip to restrain my scream of pain, and I instantly tasted blood.

The voices were above us. A shotgun blasted and the pellets rained in the high weeds not more than five feet from us.

"Boat!" I said.

"Yeah!" Kathy said back.

Then we were on the river bank and Kathy was untying a wooden row boat. I helped her push it off as best I could with my one good arm. We fell into the boat, Kathy first, me behind her. The current caught us. The current was slow, though, and I was on top of Kathy to shield her. She was shivering violently and it was hard to hold her down. She tossed her head.

"Stop!" I yelled. "What are you—?"

Then she took a bite out of my forearm.

While she moaned with satisfaction and chewed, I wailed, "Jesus! Oh, Jesus Christ! Son of a bitch!"

While she was still chewing, there was a shotgun blast and the pellets splashed in the water about a yard to our left. Then hot needles stabbed the back of my neck before I heard the blast that hit me. Kathy screamed a muffled scream beneath me and I was horrified to see blood on her back.

"Blood, Kathy! Oh god, blood! Stay still!"

She turned and looked at me, her face close. "Not mine."

"What?"

She was suddenly calm now, her eyes shining. "It's not my blood."

The current *seemed* to be carrying us along at a hundred miles an hour now, but in reality, we barely moved. The trees on the banks were a dark blur. The moon lit up the river like a spotlight.

It felt like bees were stinging me, and I had to get

away from them, so I stood up.

"No!" Kathy screamed.

And then I fell out of the boat backwards, head over heels like a diver, and sank like a rock, but I didn't care. It didn't matter. I felt nothing. Not pain. Not fear. The blue gills and catfish fled from me. The water was cloudy with mud and Jesus bugs and swirling blood.

I heard, "Hey, boy."

I continued to sink.

"Up here, boy."

Above me, floating, radiant in golden robes, was The Preacher.

And I felt a part of me powerfully pulled upward although at the same time I looked down and saw myself—my body—continue to sink in a swirl of bubbles and blood and retreating fish.

"That's it, boy. Come on. Come on now."

I rose up, and when I broke the surface of the water, The Preacher was gone. I was out of the water now, and I felt dry. When I opened my eyes, I saw the moon glistening on the surface of the river. The water was calm, smooth.

I was in the sky. Kathy was below me in the boat leaning over the side, staring at the bloody cloud in the water. I walked on the water the few feet to the boat and I stood next to Kathy, who kept peering into the river where I had fallen, and I saw that she looked different. Her complexion was gray and her face was bloated. Dark circles lay beneath her yellow eyes.

She was Dead. I could see that now.

She was Dead.

Then I saw my body surface. It was floating on its stomach, its face in the water, a hole a couple of inches below the base of its neck, blood still streaming from it. The corpse's left arm was crooked way above its head unnaturally. It—my body—was a rag doll.

Kathy reached and got hold of the cuff of its jeans and tugged it toward the boat.

She tried to get it into the boat, but she couldn't lift it high enough to get it over the side. The boat rocked and she held my body's shredded and bloody shirt to keep it with her as the boat drifted.

Kathy muttered, "Don't be dead. Don't be dead, Cadillac."

I screamed, "Preacher!" And my scream echoed across the river.

Then in an instant I was back in my body, my face in the water. I rolled onto my back, spitting river water, and grabbed the edge of the boat with both hands, and with Kathy's help, I climbed in with almost no trouble.

I looked at her. She was beautiful again.

I felt fine. Nothing hurt. I was fit as a fiddle, as the old people always said. Healthy as a horse, as Dr. Paul would have confirmed.

# AFTER

## *The Journey*

The little row boat leisurely carried us down river toward Cincinnati. We weren't far from Devil's Elbow when the air suddenly turned warm. It was July again. The air was thick with fire flies and mosquitos. I felt the heat, but I didn't start sweating from the heat and humidity. The mosquitos bit me and drew blood, but I didn't feel their sting. I thought about that, wondered what it meant, what it *would* mean.

For a while, we didn't talk. We just breathed, and the night deepened. The only sound was the lapping of water against the boat. Clouds returned and overtook the moon and the stars, and we were somewhere near the middle of the river, and we couldn't see either bank. For a long time, there were no lights on the shores or at least we couldn't see them. A fog rose from the waters, and our blindness was no longer black but white.

Kathy and I sat close, enshrouded in the cottony

fog. The only thing we could see was each other.

"Do I look different to you?" I asked.

"You're wet. Like a drowned rat." She even smiled a little when she said that.

"How 'bout my arm?"

"It looks okay."

"I think it's broken, but I can use it." I turned. "Do I have a hole in my back?"

"No. Not that I see."

"I should have a wound. I did have one. I saw it." I shook my head. "It doesn't hurt, though."

I could see where she had bitten me on my forearm, but I didn't want to bring *that* up. Maybe she was embarrassed. Maybe she didn't even remember doing it.

"Do I look the same?" she asked.

I studied her face. "Back there, when I first came out of the water, you didn't. But just for a minute. Now you look the same. You look pretty as ever."

She smiled, her face radiant through the mist, her eyes bright with her own internal light. She said, "You look pretty as ever too."

\*\*\*

At a marina on the Newport, Kentucky, side of the

river across from Cincinnati, under the cover of darkness and fog, we traded our rowboat for an aluminum motor boat I hotwired. After an hour or so passed, and our fear of being caught by the river patrol and tossed in prison or reform school diminished, we started enjoying the speed and the wind and even the buzz of the motor in our ears as we made our way toward Cairo, Illinois. Kathy's hair blew back straight from her head. She looked like a goddess.

The fog lifted before daybreak, and the sky was clear. I cut the engine along a wilderness stretch of the river, and we drifted to shore. We sat on the river bank and watched the brilliance of the sun rise. The river became a ribbon of gold winding through the lushly green landscape.

I looked at the sun on Kathy's face, and she looked beautiful to me, but I knew now how she looked to others—the puffy face, the dark gouges under yellow eyes—and I had some idea of how I would look now to others. When we heard the sounds of motor boats, we stepped into the woods and stayed hidden there throughout the day, exploring. The animals and birds got quiet in whatever part of the forest we entered. We came upon a couple of old camp fires, the sites littered with beer cans.

Around the time the sun was directly overhead, we came upon a clapboard hunting cabin. I had my Swiss Army knife and unscrewed the latch holding a small lock. The one-room cabin was stocked with jugs of drinking water and sacks of cornmeal and canned corn and canned green beans and canned tomatoes and pork and beans and cans of coffee. There was a stack of *Penthouse* magazines in a corner and boxes of rifle cartridges. There were three oil lamps and two metal-frame beds. We had no desire to sleep or to eat, but we did have a desire for each other.

I think now—here I am, having walked this earth for sixty-five years—it was strange we didn't need sleep; we didn't need food; but we needed each other desperately. It occurs to me that it was a perfect romance. Young lovers often lose their appetites and stay awake long hours, subsisting on each other. But such a scenario lasts only briefly for most couples. For me and Kathy, nothing has changed in half a century.

Toward evening, we made our way back toward our motor boat. We were relieved that it was still there, tied up at the bank and camouflaged with some cattails and small tree branches. We sped through the early darkness until we saw a small marina where we could exchange boats. We always left a boat when we took a new one. That way, it felt like we had stolen only one boat. Eventually, people would get their boats back, we rationalized, and ultimately, we would leave our last boat to be found too, so in the end, we would not have stolen anything—we would have only *borrowed*. If we had had any money, we would have left it to pay for gas, but in 1971, gasoline cost about thirty cents a gallon, so our use of the gas was only petty theft.

Kathy and I shared the desire—or need—to be as good as we could. We didn't talk about it, but we knew that eventually we would start doing things we might feel guilt over. Necessary things. Uncontrollable things.

***

Just past Lake Village, Arkansas, Kathy admitted she was awfully hungry. Her face was drawn and pale. She quivered and moaned, clutching at her stomach. It was near dawn, and we were drifting out of gas near the river bank. About a hundred yards up ahead, a trash dump was burning, black smoke rising from car tires into the sky and dissipating across the water toward the Mississippi side.

I cut the engine, and we slowly drifted toward the

burning trash dump, and we saw that there was a smaller fire near it. A grizzled gray-haired man in a ragged gray suit way too big for him sat hunched at the little campfire, holding in the flames a stick speared through some kind of small animal. His hair stuck out on either side of his skull like horns.

As we were passing him, he started gnawing on the little roasted corpse. It might have been a rabbit, but for some reason, it looked like the carcass of a cat.

Kathy peered toward the hobo. "I've been hungry for so long."

She rocked back and forth, trembling, moaning softly.

"I know."

I looked back at the hobo, who was behind us now. "I'm starting to feel kind of hungry too."

Trash floated in the water. Plastic milk jugs. Diapers. Broken toy parts. A flattened box from Colonel Sanders floated by. Kathy hung her head and then lifted it just enough to look at me with raised yellowish eyes. "I'm not hungry for chicken. I don't want no Colonel Sanders."

"I know."

"You know?"

"Yeah."

"Or Burger King Whoppers."

"Yeah."

"Or fries or beans or bread or . . . or ice-cream!" The word "ice-cream" came out as a kind of shriek.

"Yeah, I know."

"Or . . . ."

"Me neither."

I steered the boat to shore. The sky was starting to lighten on the horizon, but it was still pretty dark.

As we walked toward the hobo, I watched him closely, his campfire illuminating him. I knew that a man like him could be dangerous. A man like him had nothing to lose and could not afford affection, sympathy, or compassion for anyone. His fingers pinched like claws over his hunk of meat—whatever it was. He was a man who wouldn't think much about smashing somebody's head in with a steel pipe.

I noticed a piece of drift wood, about three feet of three-inch-thick tree branch. I picked it up. When we got close to him, he gazed up at us with blurry eyes. A whiskey bottle lay beside him. He sneered. "This ain't no party. You kids get outta here, I'll cut ya!" He pulled a long steak knife out of his coat. "I'll gut ya both like fish. So get outta here now. This is *my* place."

We stepped into the light of his campfire, and his face changed. He squinted and then his rheumy eyes got big. "Jesus, what the hell happened to you two freaks? It ain't Halloween!"

I stepped closer and raised the tree branch over my head. He tried to scramble to his feet and slash out with the knife at the same time. I sidestepped him and brought the branch down, the blow glancing off the side of his head just above his ear, and he dropped onto his knees. His breath was coming fast and raspy. I smelled whisky and his body odor—a combination of sweat, motor oil, rancid meat, and sewage. The roasted carcass he was eating lay on the ground now at the edge of the campfire, and more than ever it looked like a cat.

He spit at me, and as he lunged at me with the steak knife, I swung, catching his arm. He grunted and dropped the knife. When he bent for it, I hit him on the back of the head. He fell, sprawled face down into the mud, and Kathy—without hesitation and with a ferocity that surprised me—grabbed the knife and plunged it into the back of his neck.

\*\*\*

Twenty minutes or so later, we were back in the boat, drifting, and the sun was breaking on the horizon to our left, the light of a new day shimmering across the water.

"We had to do it," she said. Her face was no longer drawn or pale. She breathed easily. She looked gorgeous. Her lips were kind of puffy and red, like she'd applied lipstick.

I leaned toward her and kissed her and tasted blood.

"Yeah," I said. "We had to."

"He wasn't a nice man."

"No. He was . . . he was an *ass*hole."

"Yeah."

The sun rose higher and it was a bright day, but in the distance up ahead there were storm clouds moving upriver toward us.

"Cadillac."

"Yeah." I felt the storm's cool wind on my face, and it felt good.

"Only assholes."

"What?"

"Only assholes. Okay? That's going to be our rule."

"Sure."

"You really think we can stick to that? Just assholes?"

"Sure. World's got plenty of assholes. I don't think

we'll run short.

# TODAY
## The City of Bones

At night, regardless of the weather, Kathy and I set up on a street corner and perform music. The tourists tend to be drunk and loud and just stagger past us, maybe hooting like football fans or howling like dogs on a full moon or giggling like the sorority girls some of them are, but a few stop for a while. They stare. They listen.

We bill ourselves as "The Dead Kids." We have t-shirts showing our own gruesome faces. Kathy plays electric keyboard and I play acoustic guitar. Our songs are soft, slow, like the opening to Led Zeppelin's "Stairway to Heaven" or folksy, melancholy like Bobbie Gentry's "Ode to Billie Joe." And we do The Doors' "Riders on the Storm."

For long stretches, we close our eyes and improvise. We play something that sounds bluesy but also classical but also country. It's all instrumental (except for occasional soft sighs). It's eerie and peaceful. People ask us what it is, and we say it's "The Magic Death Blues."

We never play the same thing twice. Only the mood repeats. We want to convey to people the peace that we feel—most of the time. Occasionally, at the end of one of these improvisations, I leap in the air and start smashing my wooden guitar against the sidewalk, swinging it against the concrete again and again until it's nothing but splinters. Some people cheer and applaud. Some are frightened off. When I'm spent and satisfied, I always mutter, "That's the show, folks." And Kathy folds up the legs of her keyboard, and I gather up all the fragments of my guitar I can carry, and we walk home.

*** 

The world nowadays—the third decade of the twenty-first century—is full of magic: robots that can clean your house and serve you tea, GPS, Smart Phones, Smart Watches, cars that park themselves, cars that drive themselves, laser eye surgery, artificial limbs better than the real thing . . . . The technology we used to marvel at or laugh at when we watched TV shows like *Star Trek*, *The Jetsons*, and *The Twilight Zone* have become reality. A Dick Tracy watch used to seem so ridiculous.

Kathy and I deal in magic, but not the technological kind.

We got hold of some money (I won't go into the details, but somebody had more than enough and had come by it wickedly) and started an occult shop in the French Quarter in a city that sits atop mounds and mounds of bones. You can't dig a swimming pool or a barbeque pit or the foundation for a house in New Orleans without turning up a human skeleton or more likely a whole pile of them. It's like the whole place is built on a mass grave.

Devil's Elbow had some things in common with The French Quarter—a freakishness and proximity to death, a high percentage of alcoholism, suffocating humidity—but there's gaiety here that we rarely saw back home and an insidious quality to the evil that makes it harder to discern. In Devil's Elbow, you knew who was a mean drunk or who would shoot you or knife you for ten cents and who beat his wife and kids, who was feebleminded, who was harmless, who was generous to a fault. Here, it's not so easy to tell.

Kathy and I sell pre-prepared potions, amulets, t-shirts (our "Dead Kids" t-shirts are very popular), stones with magical properties, jewelry, and books about witchcraft, aliens, near-death experiences, Bigfoot, the Loch Ness Monster, New Age health remedies, haunted houses, reincarnation, and astral projection. We also sell a book I published a couple of years ago. It's called *Devil's Elbow: July 3, 1971*, and everybody thinks it's fiction.

We burn incense and play The Doors or music from the Far East or our own recordings or what's supposed to be soundtracks of alien communications captured by NASA. A lot of the tourists roll their eyes at our merchandise. Some giggle. But some take the shop very seriously—they enter the shop the way people enter a church. Some stay for hours. Some spend a lot of money.

After five decades, Kathy and I still look the same, eternally sixteen. We look fine to each other, but we don't forget that we don't look fine to others. We wear Halloween make-up to give the impression that our look is entirely intentional. People call us the "Goth Kids," if not "The Dead Kids," and long-time neighbors assume, I guess, that we've aged under the make-up.

Most of our neighbors from when we first moved in have moved away or died by now. One long-time neighbor, who has now passed away, called us "The

Dick Clark Kids" because it seemed to him we were eternally youthful, the way *American Bandstand*'s Dick Clark seemed for decades.

In the occult shop and in the French Quarter in general, nobody really notices much or cares. After all, there's a seven-foot man who lives just a few doors down from us who struts around every day bare-chested and wearing a hula skirt, eye-shadow, rouge, and lipstick. He's the only of our neighbors who calls us "freaks," but he calls everyone freaks, especially the rich college kids who come for Mardi Gras or Spring Break. He flips his long bleach-blond hair over his beefy shoulder, sneers, and shouts at them, "Have some decency for Christ's sake!" They laugh and snap his picture with their iPhones. "Asshole!" he shouts. "You owe me five bucks for that picture you just took, asshole."

Like any place else, New Orleans is full of assholes.

Every once in a while a tourist — some blue-haired Baptist church lady, usually — will stop us on the sidewalk and, with a wagging finger and a sad, turned-down lower lip, will tell us we'd be nice-looking children and could possibly save our souls if we cleaned ourselves up. We nod politely and thank her for the good advice. Such people are safe from us.

They're the wrong kind of asshole.

The right kind of asshole is the kind who comes into the shop wanting poison or anything else that will kill somebody—maybe his ex-wife or ex-girlfriend or his boss or some neighbor with a poodle that yaps too much. We smile as though we have complete sympathy with his need to put his mother in a coma so that he can get hold of her credit cards or make a co-worker's penis fall off or have a heart attack so that some new secretary or promotion can be his. We nod as he rails about the money he has to pay his ex-wife. Sometimes a customer just wants complete power over an innocent victim—maybe a young woman in his office or his apartment building who absolutely refuses to get naked for him. More often than not, as he talks, it becomes clear he has a long list of people he wants dead, in a coma, paralyzed, in acute pain, or naked.

Kathy and I just need to glance at each other to confirm our agreement, our perceptions, and our judgment.

We tell him we have exactly what he needs. Because of its delicate composition and illegal nature, it's "secured" in the backroom, we whisper to him. We tell him he'll just need to follow us. We put the "closed" sign on the front door.

My heart barely speeds up, I'm so used to the routine now. Kathy still gets a little breathless and will emit a strange hysterical laugh before she can contain herself.

A five-inch-thick two-hundred-year-old black-painted oak door separates the shop from the backroom. It has iron hinges and a padlock on the shop side. I carry the key for the padlock. Kathy carries the skeleton key for the original deadbolt lock. We keep the hinges oiled, so it opens silently. No creaks. No squeaks.

When we lead our customer into the backroom, we pull the string on a single bare light bulb that hangs from the ceiling, and it swings blindingly, shadows shuffling here and there. Our customer blinks several times. He might shiver because of the chill the room always holds.

We gently push the thick door shut, slide the metal bar that secures it. A hidden mechanism inside the thick oak automatically falls into place with a heavy clank. Soldiers with a battering ram couldn't break down that door.

There are no windows. The walls are made of foot-thick timbers and concrete blocks and are lined with old pine library shelving. The shelves are not stocked with books but with jars and bottles—an inventory of roots and herbs, some of which we grow in our courtyard, some we order from China and Mongolia and Turkey and Hungry and South Africa and Peru. (Miss Trout would be impressed with what we've accumulated and the level of expertise we have achieved.)

But we don't bring this particular customer back here for the roots and herbs. Against one wall is a long porcelain sink over a hundred years old and as big as a bathtub. It has two ancient spigots, one for cold water and one for hot. They squeal horribly when turned, and the pipes inside the walls suck air, gasp, and clang in misery.

In one corner is a gas stove from the 1940s that has been cold the forty-some years we have lived here. At the center of the room is a large butcher-block table. Lying in the center of it are a large meat cleaver and a long carving knife with a marble handle. The floor is concrete, and there's a drain in the center, so it's easy to clean.

I mentioned that The Quarter is built on a mass grave. Our courtyard is full of bones.

Our customer says, "Cool room. You got other

rooms?"

"No. Just the main shop and this," Kathy says.

"You live somewhere else in The Quarter?"

"No, we live here."

The customer blinks. "So where you sleep?"

"Oh, we never sleep."

The customer laughs a little, says, "Okay." We laugh too.

Nodding at the old stove, the customer says, "Hey, man, this is your kitchen?"

"Yeah."

"You kids, like, eat in here?"

Kathy and I look at each other.

Kathy emits that strange, hysterical laugh, then says, "Yeah, we, like, eat in here."

CPSIA information can be obtained
at www.ICGtesting.com
Printed in the USA
FSHW011938211019
63259FS